1

Prologue...5
Chapter 1 9
Chapter 2 39
Chapter 3 59
Chapter 4 79
Chapter 5 101
Chapter 6 119
Chapter 7 139
Chapter 8 159
Chapter 9 175
Chapter 10 191
Chapter 11 205
The end.....................................215

Prologue

'Watches aren't what they used to be,' she said, looking admiringly at her own feet. Her feet were her livelihood, she had added. They weren't pretty feet. They were ugly and gnarled.

'They are not full of the same distracting passion I'm used to. They're supposed to keep me lover's thoughts occupied while I go through his pockets with my toes, without him noticing. My lover is supposed to be blind with jealousy after seeing the watches' passion for me. Stop laughing. There'll be no laughing under me own roof, except me own, so shut up.'

Rene tried to stifle her giggles. The woman didn't inspire passion. She inspired adverts for corn plasters and mental health posters.

The peeling nail varnish showed the yellowing toenails underneath.

'Supposed to be blind with jealousy or rage,' she repeated 'so's they can't see what's under their noses years later. I tell yer, when they look back, they'll blame the innocent, like I did. Ha ha. Of course, I *could* have been doing a bit of caressing with me feet, instead, and using me hands in his pockets.'

She inspected her feet again and bent one knee, to pick a piece of blistered skin off her heel. 'And I'd fool him it was the cat scratching him when I did this.' She quickly kicked forward and up, hitting out at an imaginary enemy, with a rough, uneven toe nail.

'The real Watches have always been on the quiet side. They used to live in the woods. They lived in the woods so long, they'd forgotten how to speak. Proud they were. Too proud to pass the time with the likes of us. That was before me time.' She frowned, looking slightly confused for a second or two before hackingly laughing. 'Watches. Time. Did you hear what I said ? If you want to hear more you'll have to pay me. Me oldest even has to pay to talk to me, and she's me daughter, so don't think I'll let you off.'

She waited for a few minutes, and seeing that she wasn't going to get any money, and that her audience was losing interest, she continued from another direction. Something would interest this mean girl.

'Oh, alright then you've twisted me arm. Better than me neck. Ha ha. That's why the wood-dwellers became known as 'watches', because they watch from the wood. They don't talk with their tongues, see? They talk with their eyes. They'd look at a child's wrist as if they were turning it over, and then they'd look at me great gran's hand. They were quiet, so they didn't disturb the animals, she told me, and it became a habit. My gran took offence to that, when they didn't speak to her either. It was like she was another animal to them.'

She stopped, coughed again, and looked for a response. When Rene still didn't respond, she continued talking, but inclined her head slightly towards Rene's pocket.

' Me great gran said that they wanted to wring the neck of her child. That was a joke and a half, cause that was the furthest from their minds. She then said he'd came into the village, wanting to swap his earth turn: his veggies, but that was what her mind was on; the child's uses. A chicken looks like a wee babe, once its plucked of its feathers, and she thought that is what he dealt in – babies and chickens. How was she to know, without him saying?' The old woman paused, her interest now being caught by her own lively hands, which were acting out her words, before adding; 'So he was as much as saying to me great nan, who'd never fetched or carried in her life, her being known as lascivious, that he had some tatties left over if she'd like to swap something of use. Course, another view was that he was saying that he didn't like being watched by her, not one little bit. Anyway, she blamed him, see, afterwards, when the babies disappeared. He put the idea in her mind, if nothing else, she had said. After that, after all the rumours were started, the Watches never come near her again, but watched from the woods with anger and hatred in their eyes. But he wouldn't have known that, my great gran's fella wouldn't have. She would have told him a heap of lies to keep him nervous and interested; like how the Watches secretly loved her but she was forbidden to the likes of them, like how they were too dirty for her type. That's how our own Watches became invented. They watch for us, now, and are what we pretended they were, as long as we pay them. .. *and* people used to think we owned a watch, when we talked about them. Watches were expensive in those days, so that made us look as if we worth money. Of course, my great gran's fella became one as well, after she robbed him up – A real Watch, not one she paid. He'd stand around waiting for his chance to get his revenge, and then she would say he was mad with passion for her too. See, I bet you didn't know that, for all your fancy words... How they came about. Oh, now I see what you're getting at, so you 're saying that's why we changed the second letter of 'watches' to an 'I'; so it was witches and not watches. I get yer. To save confusion. But we likes confusion, or don't you understand, else we wouldn't get away with it. It's the likes of you that changed it. To that. No. We are Switches, but you can't see the 'S'. It is inside of us.' She reached out for her hand cream. She squeezed some into her palm, and gently rubbed it in her dry skin. 'That's for me sole skin. Sold skin? Do you get it? There's me s'old feet, my sold meat.? I never go to reunions, me, I don't.'

Rene hadn't said anything. The old woman was trying to make her look confused, and was trying to shock her. She was probably filming her with a webcam, ready to add words and actions later.

She knew Switches weren't that but she wasn't going to say. Switches were people who looked identical, swapped places, *and* stood around looking at people with their talkative eyes. Witches were people who had characteristic faces – big noses and slanty eyes who talked a lot and generally avoided mad old women with foot fetishes. Rene thought that witches were less vain with their looks too, and didn't care about the wrinkles that smiling and talking apparently gave, so weren't as silent as the Switches. Uncle Arthur was a witch. She herself was a Switch. She wasn't vain – she had to keep her looks as youthful as possible for her swaps to work – but she knew people who were silent because of wrinkling skin.

'You off? Already? Sit yourself back down before you goes to her down the road. She'll lie about me, she always has done. I got to keep my tools of me trade well oiled. No wonders some went mad when they 'eard that's what you does to yer machines.' Said the old woman.

Chapter 1

Arthur thought it was going to be a difficult day when he saw Henry at their usual meeting place. Henry was bent over double, talking between his legs, and Henry didn't normally do things like that.

A difficult day for Arthur is when he had to be diplomatic to people who were familiar-looking, but unknown to him. He would have to stay silent and watch for personality leaks and character eruptions, and that was a complex thing for Arthur to do. Also he would have to turn his mobile on and get a photo to send to his Henry, and the phone was in his back pocket. He would have to put one hand on his hip, and sneak it out in a 'my back-is-hurting' type of way, making him look as suspicious as the knee-starer in front of him.

His Henry did things that were less noticeable. Other witches did the 'centre of attention' thing, in the hope that by welcoming attention they would receive less of it.

This way of thinking seemed to do with bullying and psychology. If there was someone in the centre of things already then bullies hopefully wouldn't bother to surround anyone. Arthur presumed they thought there was already a bullying happening that they couldn't see – they would avert their gaze if some harassment was occurring as they didn't want to witness bullying because when they were bullying they didn't want witnesses.

.

The witches were normally the ones to put themselves in the centre, but, admittedly, that could be due to them hearing excessive rumouring about themselves being put on bonfires and not due to every day bullying. There was a huge difference between the two, and he wouldn't accuse a bully of being a bonfire builder unless the bully was armed with tinder wood, a lighter, and a knife and fork.

And perhaps a pitchfork as well.

Witches who did that sort of thing liked to stand where they presumed a bonfire would have been built in the past and liked to wave their arms about in fire like impersonations. Arthur guessed they liked to think they were there instead of a bonfire and that they were like a preventative to hoards starting one.

They were quite annoying and it was anyone's guess which came first – the witch on the bonfire, or the witch impersonating one. Arthur supposed that habitually trying to get everyone's attention could be more than irritating to people walking past but it wasn't an exclusive habit to witches.

Switches did it a lot too, as did emergency services, teachers and sportspeople, and all for different reasons.

It was hard to tell the difference between all of them though because, unlike witches, they were all very similar looking to each other.

Habitual centring for witches didn't really work as Arthur had noticed that the bullies, who normally couldn't admit they were wrong, vindicated their opinion of bigger bullies being around by placing bundles of firewood in the precise place that a witch had previously been standing in before, before quickly running in the opposite direction, skidding to a halt, and averting their gaze again.

It normally didn't take long for someone to step into the same space.

The bullies would then saunter past one more, smugly.

It seemed to be just witches that were persecuted and Arthur thought it strange that it was them as they were un-enviable, inedible, and not competition. Arthur thought the hostility was to do with witches being harder to swap than the plainer Switches but it could have been their personality.

Switches tended to be uniformly plain and swapped places frequently, hoping no one would notice the deception. They thought that it couldn't happen with witches. They had told him so.

Arthur thought the Switches didn't get out much, or didn't see enough even though they looked enough, as he was standing with someone who might or might not be Henry.

Henry had nothing that a Henry double would want, Arthur thought. He had no wealth, property, reputation or prettiness the Switches could use but he had forgotten what some of them could be like. Some had a psychotic insistence that they were everyone to everybody. It was something to do with wanting to-get-their-own-way, if other-people were-getting-their-own-way. This seemed reasonable, but they didn't seem to quite understand why they shouldn't have someone-else's-own-way. If a baby was having a nappy changed the adult Switches would insist they wanted the same and would buy some nappies. They would wait to be changed with a sulky determined look on their faces.

Arthur sighed. It wasn't something he wanted to think about but Switch motive involved the person who he was looking at.

The Henry that Arthur was staring at seemed to be trying the quick-switch method of ID theft. This involved doing something unusual and out of character so Arthur would notice the action the man was making rather than concentrating on his facial features.

Arthur squinted his eyes, hoping he looked stern and un-understanding.

The Henry twin also looked as if he had mixed the Henry name with Arthur's, as if he wasn't sure which name belonged to which person. He was bent over, in a sort of 'Half – er' way, ready to imply he was Arthur, as well, if that was the man's name.

Arthur could imagine him at the police station, 'no officer, no. This is *my* bank card. They call me Arthur as well, because of the way I stand. Look –there is 'Half –her', they say as I hobble past'…' He probably wore a bra on his bum too, when everyone was looking, for the 'her' he imagined was part of an Arthur name. As he had thought before, Switches were very unrealistic in their conviction, but *they* thought they were convincing.

Perhaps he thought he was being *persuasive* by involving Arthur's name in his charade.

With Arthur it had the opposite affect. He had never been in love with his mirror, due to him being ugly, so was never persuaded by people who looked like him, were called the same name as him, or by people who acted his name out.

He looked at Henry again.

Then Henry spoke, 'and don't look at me like that Arthur. You should know me by now. I am checking my legs to see if I am victim of a curse. She went too far this time.'

Arthur looked at him. He didn't believe a word.

He crouched down until his face was level with Henry's upside down one, reaching for his mobile phone at the same time.

'What did you say Henry? I didn't quite catch that.'

'I said, Arthur that she went too far this time.'

Arthur looked at him carefully. The art of being a good friend is to not give an impersonator any ideas of what kind of person your friend is.

He kept his face non-committal, but raised an eyebrow, swivelled his head round, and held it upside down, so Henry could see he was eye-brow raising.

Henry narrowed his eyes in annoyance. 'Miranda. Miranda went too far; and not too far away from me.'

He knew his granddaughter's name, so it could be him talking. If it was, Arthur would like to know why he was making himself look like an idiot.

Perhaps it was still about Arthur's name though. Arthur's name may have finally influenced him. So many people were name-stealers, by actions, if not in deed, that it could catch up on the real owner of it, eventually.

Misusing a person's name was a way to make a person change it, or not to mention it in public, so it could be used by a criminal instead.

Arthur was always haunted by younger look-a-likes, in the past,calling them selves his name by acting like a female body part, in the most derogatory way. Luckily, their female relatives had finally stopped raising their skirts every time he walked past, but Arthur had felt the urge, years later, to put a kilt on, and to do the high land fling. Henry had always been by his side, receiving the same unwanted information from them.

But there had been lots of Henry impersonators too. Perhaps Henry was being 'Hen-me.' Arthur supposed he could be acting in a hen-like way too. They both were. Arthur still had his hand in his back pocket, making a wing of his arm.

He understood about what Henry was saying about cursing but one familiar sentence wasn't going to appease him.

Curses were like tourist persuasion (trying to make something very un attractive into something worth visiting, buying or donating to.) They took a lot of time and mostly worked when the victim was feeling weak, or discontented with other human beings. He and Henry always directed curses towards their legs when they felt they were being cursed: Legs were strong and couldn't reach, like hands would. Most curses were nods in the wrong direction, and involved looking at hands, and insinuating the hands were doing something they shouldn't.

Years of being cursed could finally make a person do something they didn't want to, by sheer subconscious direction.

Legs just stood, or walked.

They bent or didn't bend.

They were easier to control than fidgety hands and bored faces. They didn't react so independently.

Another thing that worried Arthur was that Henry wasn't normally that annoyed about Miranda. He had become used to her, over the years. But perhaps that his annoyance proved it was Henry. A fake Henry would probably have just repeated Henry's gruff 'oh it will blow over,' type of comment, or even Henry's 'can't wait until she moves out,' sort of remark.

He wouldn't have been so... original.

Switches, as a rule, were never original.

Arthur tried a squinty eyed look again. 'We fishing?' he asked.

Not that they actually fished, but they gave the appearance of fishermen. They had waders and fishing nets. They had lots of green clothes and flat cap hats. If they didn't turn up to fish, someone who actually killed the fish would take their place, and Arthur didn't want that to happen but if Henry said 'yes' then he knew it wasn't Henry, but an imposter, who would actually fish. They always went not-fishing on a Monday.

'Friday already?' Henry replied.

Arthur relaxed. That was Henry's safe reply, should Arthur ever have to ask him about when they didn't fish.

It *was* Henry, bending there.

He waited until Henry had straightened up before giving him another quick look. 'So Henry, what did Miranda do to make you so annoyed? Not once, Henry, in all these years I have known you, have you stood in the street with your head between your legs. What did she do?'

14

Henry sighed, in an over-exaggerated breathe. Come to think of it, thought Arthur, he *was* quite hen-like too now. Perhaps he had grown into his name without Arthur noticing. Henry's mouth became quite tight and puckered and his jowl lines gave the appearance of the rest of a beak. His little eyes became smaller and because his white hair was flattened back in a quiff-type hairstyle it was also similar to the swept back feathers of the bird. Arthur made a mental note to check his own face for fowl jowls. He may have saggy breast cheeks, without even knowing about it. 'Half-her'… he dragged the name out, in his thoughts while nodding at Henry, in an understandable way, as Henry explained. Arthur also listened for a chicken-type sound, in case Henry had been the delayed victim of a namist attack. No chicken-like sound could be heard. Shame, really, he hadn't heard a chicken-like sound for years, so it would have been nice to be reminded what they sounded like. He hadn't heard a cow sound for years either, now he came to think of it.

Singing ' Old McDonald had a farm' wasn't the same as it used to be. There were a lot of silent gaps where there used to be animal voices.

He looked at Henry.

Arthur started to remember more about their curse avoidance. They even danced with their hands on their knees, to be absolutely sure that their legs were doing what they had asked them to do. 'I'd forgotten our fear of misbehaving quadriceps. You haven't been that distracted for a long time. Had anyone cursed your bodily parts while you were too distracted to notice?'

Henry looked down at himself with a worried frown. 'I'm not sure Arthur. My aches and pains have bounced around me for so long, that when I take notice of them they seem worse. So I am not sure Arthur. Not sure at all. My left leg seems a bit boisterous?'

Arthur sighed in a less obvious and less poultry way than Henry did. 'I think that it is more to do with your age, rather than another witch's interference. Curses *did* get out of hand for a while though, didn't they? The amount of times we used to come around that corner to find a man or woman with their feet casually relaxing on someone else's toes, as if it was normal, and as if their hands had been cursed for years. Changing it to feet certainly helped them not to make spontaneous gestures. They had to pretend that they were acting out the tidal patterns of Greece and Italy though so the Switches didn't know the curses had nearly worked. Do you remember? They loudly blamed it on the over advertising of the map, if I remember correctly. I think it *was* the map making them behave in that way as well. Not just the Switches.' He added, 'How did she offend you and Eileen? Are you calm enough to tell me about it?'

'I am not, Arthur, I am not. And the world isn't always about your atlas map. Damn it Arthur, you made me contradict an obvious truth that is a blatant lie.'

Henry then fell silent.

That was now classed as Hen-like too, Arthur supposed. Henry was making chicken noises by not making a sound.

Henry's wife, Eileen may have had a bad case of namist herself. 'I – lean'. She was a bit on the thin side now, and was angry most of the time. Now he had thought about it, he would have to have a good look at her, one day, and see if she was the Eileen Henry had started off with. He was sure she had been bigger, and lighter eyed.

Arthur wasn't a psychologist, but he thought that that woman confused 'anger' with ''unger.'

She stayed angry, most of the time.

Arthur steered Henry towards the pub, with a sort of sideways walk. Arthur wanted to find a mirror. He was getting old without realising it. He hoped he didn't have jowls *and* cheek pimples. But that would explain the 'we'll have you under arrest'

16

comments that had been directed at him and his flabby cheeks. They were saying he was breast faced, he was sure of it.

The village pub was named 'Ephphatha'. It had become a substitute church, over a period of time, because people had become quieter over the years.

Some thought it had become quieter because of the pub name, which was hard to say without spitting. It was like the owners didn't like people to talk. The threat of being put on the hearth was lurking in the pronunciation of the pub sign. Spit, spit, spit it said to communal drinkers, as if they were turning over on a grill. Not a lot of people said yes to an invite to the pub after hearing the pubs name.

Henry and Arthur generally ignored the insinuation of the what-happens-to-the-witches type of hint, which sometimes accompanied the 'Fancy a pint at the Ephphatha?' sentence. Their inherited persecution, that always seemed to involve a wood fire in the middle, had been almost forgotten with the rise of mobile phone cleansing operatives, who were now new targets for the criminals. They reputedly earned more than witches did so had the favoured status in the Switch world.

Switches in the pub were the silent watchful type who waited for drunken words to give them clues to possessions and relatives. Henry and Arthur always had a quick chat at the bar, to show they were not scared, even when they were. Lack of verbal communication, they felt, bought in more Switches, and didn't, as the landlord once explained, deter them through lack of local knowledge.

People who were quiet just got replaced quicker, without anyone really noticing, they thought.

The pub was mostly silent, nearly all of the time, as communication between customers was mostly limited to nervous nods and elbow avoidance. Even if the customers were life long friends, they couldn't say, in case one of them wasn't.

They kept chatting for the intimacy of their homes.

Henry leant across the bar and said 'Don't you think she looks like Miranda?' He said it loudly, with the intention of being overheard, which was unusual for Henry.

Arthur was surprised again, by his friend's lack of normal personality.

Henry was looking at a girl leaning across the bar opposite and re-naming her as his granddaughter. The girl was about the same age as Miranda, with the same sort of looks.

Miranda probably wouldn't agree, but Switches could be convincing in their prolonged looks in someone's direction. She may succumb to a moving mirror, eventually, if the Switch started stalking her.

Arthur had once bought a window box, because the Switches had silently insisted that he plugged his broken laptop into the back of the telly. He didn't realise that was what they were saying. He mistook their silent direction for window box planting until he actually thought about it.

The Switches relied on empathy, faux intimacy, and confusion a lot for their switches to work. The same as they did when they were hoping for a curse to work. Arthur supposed the window-box thing had been an attempt at some kind of intimacy with his lifestyle, followed by sympathetic advice. If he hadn't noticed they would have followed it up with a knock on the door. It would have taken them another week or so to move themselves in, and him out. They were like that. With Miranda, it would be pretended friendship, and a familiarity with her problems with her granddad, now he had said that.

Arthur looked at Henry. He always looked the same, so there was no sliding out of the words he had just said. His physical looks meant that a change of hair cut wouldn't work either.

Arthur looked over at the woman, and wondered if he could confuse her before she started to think she was welcome in their lives. That always seemed to work with Switches. He had used that one with his house, after the window box thingy had happened. He had tidied up, and that had confused the Switches into silent eyes. Things, people and events don't change for the Switches. If they did, they would be lost and not know how to move their eyes when joining a circle of observed-in-the-past, familiar, but unknown people for the first time. A dropped sweet wrapper stays dropped on the floor and a fat person stays fat, in their world. They despised new inventions and new conversations. They detested other people having intimacy or interests. The most repelling event for a Switch is a large wedding, where everyone knows everyone. They might be expected to talk, and of course they couldn't talk with convincing intimacy, as they were strangers to the group and only looked the same as a friend.

Henry had just told the entire pub the girl's name and appearance, so this would be trickier. The girl opposite had squinted her eyes, in a Miranda type way. She knew who Miranda was and Henry was almost inviting her to take Miranda's place in the world.

Henry felt better though. He'd wanted to do that for years.

He turned his head to Arthur, and started to moan about Miranda. He was using his eyes to communicate with, not his mouth, and Arthur hated that. It made him look gay. It was too intimate and personal.

Arthur turned his head away and sipped his coke. Normally, Arthur didn't really listen to Henry's moaning, and Henry didn't normally mind Arthur's slight absent-minded look if all he was doing was losing his temper. Henry sometimes said things he didn't mean, when he was in a mood, so he didn't particularly want Arthur to remember every word. Arthur had never tried not listening with his eyes, as Henry rarely spoke with just his eyes.

Henry had made an impression in the pub, by speaking like that.

They usually chatted about less serious things. Things like taupe paper. Or sometimes something like regional leaf mould. Arthur knew he was being a devil's advocate, but he liked to imagine that the Switches would echo his words, with their eyes only, at other people. To other people, it could mean something completely different. The world is multi lingual. For him, most of the time, it was like leaving a calendar reminder for a shopping list, because if he met the Switches somewhere else, they would use their eyes to echo the words he had spoken. They might as well repeat something useful, he thought, rather than what the football was like.

Switches were imperative for most witches, who had realised the same as Arthur, but years before. The Switches just echoed other people's words back at them. It is how the witches controlled others, when they were *those* sort of witches. All they had to say was a few words, and the words would be spread about like confetti.

Switches, and ears droppers, didn't like to think they were being used as tape-recorders or that they were helping the witches, so most witches were discreet in their mumblings.

Henry, speaking that loudly, or using eye-language, was just inviting trouble. Eye language, especially, was an open invite for anyone to communicate with. Eye people were so strange. Intimacy for them was talking, when they only gave others intimate details when they weren't talking.

Arthur would have to respond to Henry, so the pub customers wouldn't think that Henry was trying to be intimate with them, but he didn't approve. He quickly looked around before staring back at Henry.

Several people were also looking at Henry with obvious disinterested interest. Arthur went red. Miranda wasn't that bad. It was an awful thing to do – swapping her for a cheap Switch. That way of thinking would kill them all. Once you let one Switch in, it was the same as letting them all in.... before you knew it, they had made themselves into a womb broom, to sweep the inhabitants of the house out. There used to be cartoons on the telly about it…so he knew all about Switches and their intentions.

He had been lucky so far.

Well, it was more than luck. Arthur would spot it if Henry and Eileen were swapped.

It was their skin.

Easily forgettable until he remembered why they were all witches, and not Switches.

He should have made Henry take his top off when he suspected it wasn't him, instead of reaching for his phone, but that would have made him look like he was picking up men in strange positions. He would have started to be known as an action-dyslexic user of escort agencies, probably. The next time he used that road, there would possibly be a half naked man, bent backwards, waiting for Arthur to approach him with the same enthusiasm Arthur showed for Henry.

Miranda wasn't the same as them. Her skin was… well, not as noticeable. It was plain. Plain as the girl opposite, who was already busy with her mobile phone, taking photos of them, while tapping and taping with the thing.

He hoped Henry would stop the Switch, before she made it to easily- swappable skin Miranda.

He turned his attention back to Henry, who was still explaining, with a look here and there, Miranda's faults and bad manners.

It was a strange kind of baby language that Switches used, and what Henry was now using – the language that had no tongue. The Switches used it because it was only babies that Switches could convince that their lies were truths, because babies were more likely to believe them and had no experience of the world. Babies waited to hear truth.

They used the baby language on adults too, though, so the adult would be taken back to their own babyhood, and be as convinced as a baby.

It was communication without argument, when there were no words, which is probably what they liked the most. Their eyes moved quickly over faces, and, thought Arthur; they really *didn't* like a verbal reply.

Arthur could remember other times when they had nudged him with eye movements. For years a particular woman had told him, in her no-voice way that he would drop five pounds for her, and Eileen had lost even more weight instead. It was because he accidentally echoed too. That happened sometimes, with Arthur, as he tried to understand why strangers were meaningful with their eyes. His own eyes would wobble about, as he was busy doing something else. He would be making a cup of soya milkshake and be telling the kitchen cupboard about the best way to pick someone's pocket.

Another person, a man, always eye-balled Arthur with the message that he would imagine him speaking in a favourite actor's voice, when he thought of the words he was implying. This way he would be someone Arthur admired, rather than disliked. Then Arthur would do what he wanted him to do. Arthur's favourite TV personality was a cartoon, so it hadn't worked.

Switches scared him, when he thought of them too much. They were so insistent, and so uncivilised.

They reminded him of cannibals.

Only very young babies couldn't talk, and they behaved like a new born all the time, as if they were still living the same life as a newborn. It was as if their breast fed diet hadn't changed ; as if they were still eating women in adult hood. It wasn't just women that weren't safe. Men suffered from the same wide eyed gaze, aimed in their direction. The Switches that scared him implied, quite openly, that they thought penises testes were breasts. Two men, walking along together, were usually given the same treatment as women; especially if they were gay.

He wondered about all the people that went missing that were never found, and shivered.

The ones that made him think they were cannibals stared up and down from his eyeball as if it was a cooking pot being carried on a stick. The cannibal stares reached down to the top of the cheek and as high as the eyebrow above. The smile line at the end of his eyes made another line.
The three lines together were three Switches, standing around a cauldron. They seemed to want to know if he was the eye in the middle, or the Switch on the outside.
They also hinted that Switch was also an electric switch, and you should be able to turn yourself on and off.
If he said 'Switches', or 'witches', in their non-verbal baby language by just using his eyes, then it looked to him like 'eat his.'

He had never stayed standing in front of a cannibal long enough for one to tell him which Switch he thought he should be.

One hint that 'look' was 'cook' was enough for him.

A cauldron was actually coloured like a dark eye ball, which made Arthur feel a little bit sick, even though his eyes were blue. Why didn't they do cauldrons in different types of enamel, like they did saucepans? He wouldn't mistake a beige and flower pattern for someone's eye. He had a nice set of poppy patterned frying pans –why wasn't there a matching set of cauldrons with the same flowery motif?

He grimaced. It was strange, but he hadn't thought Switches were dangerous for a long while. Familiarity breeds complacency. The obvious stops being mentioned, because it is obvious.

The clowns still talked about them though.. Well, mimed about them. One hint of a cannibal in a region, and they were out with their make up bags, drawing on their black eye lines, and pulling their baby type wigs on, giving everyone the bad news.

Arthur looked nervously around, before catching sight of a mirror on the wall opposite the bar. He *was* jowled, and they *did* look like breasts. How embarrassing.

He looked back at Henry.

Switches switch. They switch everything. They switched salt for sugar, and clean washing for dirtied-on-purpose washing. It was mostly their own possessions they practised on, so it was a bit pointless, unless you liked salt in your custard rather than sugar. They were almost always bad Switches. They never switched dirty washing up for clean. They were very idiotic, especially if they ate their own cooking.

Mostly Switches were Switches because they thought that later on they would 'Switch' with someone the same, but who had a better lifestyle.

But of course, that person would have to be a Switch that switched to a better life style, or the Switch couldn't happen. A Switch wouldn't want to give up wealth and power, would they? They wouldn't just move out, and let another Switch in, so they must move up, not down? But there is only so far a face can travel in the same circle, so Arthur resumed his thinking that they didn't actually move on, but died, and were eaten.

The Switches themselves never seemed to think that anyone died being a Switch, despite the obvious meaning conveyed in some of their eyes, because they had been told they wouldn't die by someone who could only persuade babies that their words were

24

true.

Arthur guessed the person who told them this was their cult leader, who took all the money and possessions, but gave back whatever their 'twin' was thought to own. When a Switch, switched, they switched entirely, right down to the same colour socks.

Arthur imagined the cult leader to be wearing a long cloak and goat's horns. Perhaps chanting occasionally and doing a lot of arm-raising. He tried not to think of it too much, else he would get indigestion.

The cult leader *did* actually wear clothes like that. The cult members expected it, but there wasn't one cult leader, there was a lots of them.

They wore a cloak because cloaks were unisex and one size fits all. Also, they didn't want to involve buttons. Buttons led to all sorts of things – discussions about zips and pretty ribbons, for a start. Then another cult leader would introduce pockets, and perhaps some kind of cuff, then another would perhaps decide on front pleats. It was better to keep it simple before arguments about style started. It was the same with colour. They would only argue about what colour the cloak would be if they had colour. Best to keep it black. If it was a no-colour white, it might be see through, and then they would have to talk about pant lines and bra bulges, about how different department stores differ with their size labels and stuff like that. Another thing would be sabotage, of course. Switches being Switches would mean that the pocket the ceremonial dagger was usually placed would be sewn up before it was given to the next cult leader, causing even more disagreements and raised eyebrows. When Switches argued, they didn't talk. They just tried to look like breasts by being pouty mouthed, before turning away, in a ' I –am-not-going-to-feed-you-stance'. The cult leaders thought that an arrangement of awkward opposing breasts wasn't the image they were trying to convey, so avoided the arguments by avoiding anything that would cause one.

The cult leaders were the first to know about a possible Switch. They had photos of everyone in every street and recruited look-a likes that were gullible and naïve. They swapped a house owner for a look-a-like tenant, who would be rented the same property, for a while, and they swapped degree holders for a 'just passed an embroidery course' doppelganger, for jobs.

A cult leader, who was a Switch, received the text message just as Arthur had looked in the mirror. It was coincidental, and apt. She was looking at Arthur and Henry, as Arthur was looking at himself and Henry in the mirror. Synchronicity is normally planned, or habitual, so this occurrence was unusual.

The woman, the cult leader, had felt compelled to communicate, once she had read the message, and said, to no one at all; 'Oh no, not again... but I suppose we're lucky...Only twice in fifty years.'

Some Switches didn't have the same sensibilities as Witches, and after only signalling to their own 'twin' for years, any shiny surface gave them a feeling of companionship. She had spotted a spoon, so was instantly at ease, and instantly chatty, with a slither of her own face to converse to. She had said it with her eyes, but that was the point. Anyone within sitting distance could see her, and understand what she was communicating.

As a cult leader, she shouldn't be doing that.

She looked at another shiny thing, her diamond ring, and tried to remind herself of her responsibilities to her cult. She gave a thin smile. She didn't have any. They were there to support her, not the other way round. Perhaps she might retire soon though, and use her excessive chattiness as an excuse for that retirement.

Arthur jerked his head at Henry, in a let's sit down kind of jerk movement.

Arthur sort of agreed about Miranda but it hadn't been her fault when she had been a new born, even though she had been blamed because of her skin; Her mum had said she couldn't bond with her because she had been born with plain skin. 'She isn't telling me what she is thinking, so I don't like her. She is too secretive.'

She had said it where Miranda could over hear, which he thought was a bit unfair.

He had gone over to the cot, to have a quick look, to make sure she wasn't upset by her mother's comments.

Her mother was a bit strange.

There is no such thing as telepathy. There is habitual routine and spying on someone. Witches were different. Witches tended to have physical attributes that some think are an explanation of their own emotions. Miranda's mother had a dark mole on her neck. She thought this meant she should be 'frank' with others, as she associated the mole with Frankenstein. She had a bleached zig-zag shape to her hair to draw attention to the mole. The zig-zag shape was supposed to be like lightening, to fit into her idea of Frankenstein, and the end of the zig-zag pointed to the mole. This, she said, is to let others know what she was like.

It was thoughts on the outside so it was 'telepathy', Miranda's mum had said.

Miranda's mum had put the word 'telepathic' on her set of business cards, for the people she did not know, along with a giant full stop. The full stop was her mole, and on the card it was placed to look like the moon.

She was frank, and that was the end of it.

Arthur had had a quick look at Miranda. Miranda's skin had been clear and was a healthy cream. Her hair, so cute, had been a little, thin spread of blond.

He had looked into her eyes. They were the deepest grey. They had sparkled with lively curiosity. At least they had, until she had focused on him. His smile had faltered when she gave him a look of pure hate.

Her nose was small, and wart-less.

Perhaps, on reflection, Miranda had heard what her mother had just said, and had tried to fit in with her idea of communication. Perhaps, and Arthur went red at the idea, Miranda had been trying to tell him she needed her nappy changed. She was full of Hate; of ate.

But now it was years later, and he was in a pub, watching Henry's eyes bounce around his own face as if he was watching a computer game.

It wasn't his fault. A two second communication with a baby didn't set the baby's mind or personality. Even if he had spent a week or so with her, it still wouldn't be his fault. He wasn't her mum, or her grand parents. He was just a family friend.

Anyway, she hadn't needed her nappy changed when she was five years old, and had bit him. Nor did she need her nappy changed when she refused to sit at the family dinner table. Miranda never ate with her family, but sneaked off, as if they were Switches, not witches. They didn't pollute their own water supply like the Switches did, so he didn't understand her reluctance to share food with them.

And her attitude was abysmal. She didn't contribute to making any household mess, but didn't help with any of the chores either. She wasn't like a Switch, or a witch. She was more like an awkward customer in a shop. Her unsaid criticism could be seen from a distance, and her scorn for their lifestyle was obvious.

28

Arthur looked at Henry. Henry was saying all that, in no-speak-hear-with-your-eyes-language.

Arthur would have to concentrate a bit more, else he would be mind-melded to Henry's feelings.

Arthur didn't actually mind Miranda much. He didn't have to live with her, like Henry did.

Miranda had lived at Henry's for years, since she was toddling about looking up people's nostrils. Miranda couldn't understand why her nearest relatives were proudly witches. She had seen the fairy tale books and hadn't liked them at all. They were hideous creatures, so why did they expect her to like them? Uck.

Eventually, and quickly, she decided it must be the nasal connection that made them think they were the same.

Arthur knew this. Miranda had been verbally very concise and clear about her thoughts.

Miranda thought they couldn't possibly identify with the rest of the books - arson, poaching and being nasty to children.

It was their noses.

She would shrink their common bond by zooming in on the nose, anyway, before they made fools of themselves by leaping about, and trying to cast spells instead of horse shoes.

The book witches, the ones that had been read to her as bed time stories, must have been really stupid Switches, and not witches like them at all, she had insisted.

The book witches had just taken the blacksmiths place and had waited for precious metal to be put in their hands. She could tell, their arms were contorted into waiting-for-something-to-be-put-in-to-them positions. They wore black, to insinuate soot covered clothing, and probably had hidden name badges with 'Smith' written on them, on the off-chance that someone would ask them who they were.

They hoped they would only have to wait for 'a spell', a spell meant a little bit of time, before they conned everyone out of their metally possessions. The only problem being that they were situated in the middle of a wood, where no-one but the robbers would pass.

The book was obviously a warning for people with low IQ's, not to take other people's places in the world.

After they had done a bit of ID theft, in the book, they normally went onto annoy small children.

She wanted all her witch relatives focus to be on the noses of the book witches, so they wouldn't be over influenced by reading a book to her. If they read a witch story to her often enough then they might turn evil, and be like the Hansel and Gretel witches.

Noses were safer. Witches noses were like carrots, so had a vegetarian-type association, instead of the child-eating type of connection that the whole witch persona could give.

She had stared at nostrils and carrots with the same myopic gaze, making her obvious comparison noticeable. She had hid the sun tan lotion, so noses became burnt and had once covered her mother's nose with orange watercolour paint, while she was sleeping.

Miranda's mum decided she couldn't live with such a literal child. She was a bit sensitive of her nose, anyway. She was beginning to age, and the lines on her nose *did* make it look more like a carrot. A vertical carrot, standing on it's end, and she *did* have a single hair growing from the middle of her forehead, as if it was the stringy bit of the bottom of a carrot, and perhaps she had neglected her nostril trimming lately, but how rude of her child to point all that out to her.

She decided that Miranda could go and live with Henry and, after advising him to hide all the baby witch books, gave him a 'How to draw realistic faces with grade C charcoal,' book to read to her instead.

That might help her to develop a bit of a physical characteristic herself, when she got older, she had thought.

Miranda had felt relief when she went to live with her grandparents, but only for a little while. After the first few months she realised that she was in the house of the people who raised her mother to believe in all that witch nonsense, and soon resorted to her usual bad behaviour.

She extended it to school, when she realised that there was only two types of people in their particular community. Switches and witches. She didn't want to be either.

Instead she strived to be an individual. She didn't think being an individual meant she had to be well behaved but she never disobeyed the law either. She spent the evenings deciding on how she would get noticed the next day. Mostly it was through bloody minded awkwardness and making sounds like an overweight bird. The sound was a sort of in appropriate laughter, which would teach a mimic – a Switch - the opposite of what she was really like. That way she figured that years later, when she heard it, she would know who stalked her and had planned to take her place.

Arthur himself favoured a kind of guffaw, mingled with a cough.

She would be at her fire side, knitting, and be satisfied if she heard the cackle outside, instead of her own normal laugh.

Apart from those mannerisms, she lied all of the time. It was another trap for twitches, as she called them. Switches were twitches when they tried to imitate everyone's loved ones at the same time. This normally happened at social gatherings, when they were in the presence of so many possible victims. Their faces twitched.

Miranda told so many contradicting lies to the same person, using her eyes to say one thing, her hands another, and her mouth yet another, that the Switch would start to twitch nearly the second time they met her. It happened when they tried to echo it all back to her with just their eyes.

She also lied just because she could.

From 'The Book Of Words.

'Taking it on the chin' used to mean 'hit that liar on the chin -that will stop his mouth from opening, and spreading lies. We won't hear him for a while.'

This gradually changed to its present meaning of someone who took bad news well. [Switches like to turn meanings upside down. It is a power thing and to do with reputations. Those that were once admired , will be despised, they hoped. Those that were once despised – themselves – will be admired. They *will* be respected by doing the wrong thing. It is strange that they never remembered that once they have turned the meaning around, the next lot of Switches will turn the meaning around, so they will be despised again, quite quickly. They cannot object, else they would be admitting that they had done something wrong when they changed the meaning of the words around.]'

Miranda lied so much she would have 'taken it on the chin' - the old meaning, but as she was female, it wasn't allowed. It was a pregnancy, inherited-memory-genetic-thing, as to why women where treated with a different set of morals to men.

Just like field work, like potato picking, could squash the embryo, so could thought, it was thought, so women were encouraged not to think too much about stuff. It wasn't true, of course but some people think that if Miranda was hit, the baby might hear about it, through her thoughts, as it was forming. Genes don't have morals, generally, but they are equipped for environmental survival. The baby's chin might grow bigger, to absorb impact, in case chin-hitting was an everyday obstacle.

Then, as the baby grew, it might plan retaliation on the chin hitter, thinking the act of chin-hitting was akin to walking into stray tree branches. The two ideas, connected before birth, may live in the subconscious, turning the same full grown adult into a spontaneous mad axe man, should he come into contact with the same chin-hitter face later on. It probably wouldn't be the same chin-hitter, either, but an innocent double. Life and age is like that. By the time the baby was an adult, the person who set the chain of later events into motion would be an OAP, probably.

It is a sad fact that humans set back their own society because of this type of scenario. The baby is equipped to deal with a long forgotten threat, and creates a threat, for the next generation, because of it.

But still, thought Arthur, despite her behaviour Miranda wasn't as bad as the Switches.

She didn't deserve to be harangued by a group of Miranda-shaped twins. It may teach her to be a bit careful of her words, he supposed, but sending a Switch after her was awful.

Henry didn't really understand what Switches were really like.

He lived in a Fairee tale, dream world, like them, where no one was injured or hurt. His world was full of pixies, and elves, princesses and other kind and gentle people.

Sometimes Arthur understood why he was like that.

Henry's chest skin made him slightly romantic.

It was like a flesh-coloured drawing book or an ever moving scope of natural skin tattoos. His chest was magical, showing woodland images and story book illusions. It wasn't 3D. It was a subtle arrangement of melanin.

He sometimes couldn't believe Henry's skin, when it changed.

Arthur knew he forgot about his own difference. He sometimes caught mermaids on his own shin, at the peripheral of his vision, and had to remind himself that they weren't floating in front of his leg, but were his leg.

The veins re-arranged themselves into images, and the skin scaled appropriately, in the right places. He didn't have to see his scenic skin every time he had a shave though, like Henry did.

He had felt sorry for Miranda, when she was a child, for not recognising the 'Iron' in the witches' book, which the witches seemed to be waiting for, as 'Ion's'.

Or for not realising why the drawings showed arms in the air, or legs kicked out.

They were looking at their limbs, waiting for the images to appear.

He supposed it *would* seem like a criminal hit list, if you didn't know what you were looking for; if you weren't used to seeing the skin's atoms re-arrange themselves, with thoughts appearing as pictograms.

Miranda hadn't really looked at them, so she didn't know.

He wasn't going to bear his legs at her, and Henry never took his top off if he could help it. They were still were persecuted in some places because of their looks, so mostly they hid it. Anyway, their images were not that noticeable as other witches used to be. In the past their skin used to be like they were standing by fires, with shadows dancing and playing on exposed limbs, when there was no fire.

That is why they were shown, in illustrations, with little cooking fires.

The cauldrons were added later.

The brighter the images were, the closer the witch would be portrayed nearer the fire. He and Henry would have been standing a little way off, in terms of image brightness. They

34

weren't Cinderella. You wouldn't know about theirs, unless you were looking for them

Witches being on top of the fire meant really clear picture skin, but Arthur didn't like to think of the literal people who would try and make the cartoon real, so he made the comparison of standing in the waterfall instead.

Arthur liked to think of water playing shadows on his skin, rather than fire. It was less dangerous.

.

Arthur tried to concentrate. He was bored of Henry, gibbering away, but not saying anything.

The bar seemed to be a little more crowded. Arthur hadn't heard the door open, so presumed that no one had come in. He looked around. One of the Switches was trying to nudge him out of the way so he could interpretate Henry's eye movements. Another one was standing over Henry, trying to see Arthur's face. He was a head taller than Henry.

'Henry, lets sit down,' he repeated.

Henry nodded, unaware of the subconscious interest he was causing. 'Okay Arthur. Where would you like to sit?'

The two switches shrunk back, as Arthur and Henry squeezed out of their way. They both looked. The empty tables seemed to have suddenly filled, but the silence hadn't warned them of the packed pub situation. The crowd were strictly silent.

Henry and Arthur pressed themselves onto a small square table, which only had room for two. Arthur felt like talking, in a nervous reaction to the atmosphere, and Henry would chat to him if he started to talk.

Arthur was hoping to make Henry's first words about Miranda less ominous. He wanted everyone to forget them. They were so serious with their listening. Nothing in their earshot was taken in a light hearted way. He supposed it was their way of assimilating. Talking showed difference and individuality, and was discouraged.

Ultra serious notice of Henry's words was off-putting. Normal people wouldn't take so much notice. He hated himself for thinking that. Half the people in the pub were ones that he had grown up with, and were normal, but careful. It was only a few that were probably Switches. He just hadn't liked the way that teenage woman, that Henry had looked at, had handled her mobile phone in their direction. She had flicked her hair in a Miranda like way, almost instantly, and had smiled. One perm later, and she could be her twin.

If he filled the pub with more talk they might forget the first words Henry had pointedly and loudly said.

He looked at the table mat. 'Heilophoniagain?' he read from it. Arthur sounded, if only to his own years, a little like he was pretending to be foreign. He cringed. The Switches stopped gazing at each other, and again paid attention to him and Henry.

Arthur sounded like he had already been switched. And once a person had been switched, it was an open field for the other Switches.

A Switch could swap with a Switch, but not with some one who didn't. The one that didn't was legally in his, or her, own place. The Switch that took the legal's place could be easily bullied back out.

Some Switches added a weird kind of accent, after their Switch, as if to say they weren't the same person, even if they answered to the same name, had *exactly* the same habits, clothes, and *exactly* the same lifestyle. The accent discouraged the actual family of the victim talking to the Switch. The accent was also to imply they didn't understand stalking was against the law and they didn't understand what the laws were.

The accents were obviously fake so that people who actually spoke more than one language wouldn't talk to them.

Arthur looked up at the ceiling shelf. He would have to think carefully about his next spoken set of words.

36

'Yes. Heilophoniagain is no- alcohol.'
Arthur looked at him. Henry didn't have a way with words either. Now they sounded like two fake foreigners.

He saw their audience look a little more interested, then a little confused.
Henry didn't notice.
Mistaking Arthur's frown for a questioning look, he added, 'Let me buy you another coke instead.'

And Arthur was left sitting there, facing the odd attention of the crowded nearby tables; the odd silent attention. Arthur felt very exposed.
They didn't even make a noise when they sipped their drinks or ate their crisps. He watched as one made eye contact with him. He was using one hand to silently open a packet of Shaky Shark flavoured potato crisps, while his eyes stayed staring at Arthur's own. A crisp left the packet and was in the starer's mouth without a sound. Arthur watched, in fascination, as the crisp silently, noiselessly, disappeared.

When Henry sat back down, Arthur had had enough time to think of something to make them seem more boring, less foreign and less worthy of Switch Attention. It was strange, Arthur thought, that he could never remember whether a group of Switches were female or male, or a mixture, after meeting them. He hardly ever remembered their physical looks. They were always a mass to him. Fear did that to him. It made his memory a blur.
'Did you notice the clouds on your way back from the bar, Henry? The one on the right looks like an angel. It is so apparent, that I would mistake it for a church statue.'
Henry stooped to see the cloud through the pub window.
'Yes! Very angel like…and the cloud next to it… What an extraordinary sight.'

The cloud next to the angel cloud was shaped like a dreamy face. It looked like a beautiful painting.

'Perhaps that is why the church moved over there.' Henry replied.

They always talked about the clouds, at this time of year, but as the clouds were only angel and face for ten seconds of every year, they always forgot they had already said the same the year before. They were being very switchy, but hadn't realized.

This year Arthur would remember, because the Switches weren't usually there. Arthur and Henry normally drifted in, annually, in a non committal way, just in time for the clouds to form. It wasn't important enough for them to remember, but at the same time, it was the most amazing sight the world had to offer. Remembering how many times they had had the same conversation made Arthur feel a little ill. The year before last he had been the one leaning over the table to have a quick look. Then five years ago they had sat outside for the event. One year he was drinking water, the next year an orange juice.

At that time, for those ten seconds, every year, since he was a teenager, those Switches hadn't been there.

He looked nervously around.

The Switches were all looking out of the window. Their eyes had finally stopped staring at him, and they were all staring at the same piece of sky.

The sky was kind of like Henry's and Arthur's skin. Like most witches skin. It had the same drifty, 'now you see it, now you don't' type of formations, and normally had the same clarity. It was so every day though, they forgot it.

'I wonder, Arthur,' murmured Henry, 'whether we are all human shaped because of those clouds; whether we evolved because of them.'

38

Chapter 2

Miranda had a boyfriend. She was at that age where she thought she ought to have one.

It made her look, to herself, more adult, and less lonely. She was still lonely with a boyfriend, but it was a bearable loneliness.

She wouldn't have felt the same if she had had some kind of pet or cuddly toy when she was younger, she was sure. She might have grabbed her fluffy red rucksack instead of his hand, when she had lonely moments.

She might have developed a bag fetish and felt emotion for faux fur instead of him.

She had wondered about the credibility of people who claimed to have a stronger attachment to soft toys. She didn't really feel she could trust someone who grabbed their teddy in an emergency.

Her boyfriend was named Graham.

Graham was average shaped, with average features. Miranda sometimes thought he was a Switch, because he sometimes looked better-looking in a certain light. He also sometimes looked thinner, and on a rare occasion, he looked just not like himself.

Switches started their switching young.

It was stupid of him if he did, and a bit gay. Men who were Switches only really got close to their own image. They only had self adoration. Girlfriends were just referred to as their mothers, and that idea made her feel a bit unwell. Mothers provided their meals, and she didn't want to be someone's midnight snack.

That is all she could think of, when she thought of Switches and their relationships. She spent a lot of time on the peripheral of other people's conversations, so she mostly guessed it was the general opinion of most.

Part of her felt sorry for them. She felt an empathy, but only sometimes, like when she thought of Graham.

And sometimes, when she compared their lifestyle to her own, she could understand why they disappeared into their 'twin' cities. She would have disappeared too, she supposed, if she'd had to stay with her mother. She could imagine the safety of being part of a lonely crowd, but to her they were more like a sub-human tribe.

In fact, once they had found a face the same as their own, they behaved as if a differing face was potential food. If they didn't have a differing face, they bullied the smallest of their own, in case they got hungry later. She had seen it at school. Can-be bully, they were. She used to call their smallest look-a-likes, 'pocket mirrors'. The older twins would sneak off to stare at the youngest twin, and be full of self-criticism for what they saw as the littlest one's faults.

'Myra' was one of their collective names, so they knew what sort of group they were all in. 'The hall of mirrors', they had called themselves originally. 'Myras' was easier to write on the notepads and in their mobiles than 'accumulated faces that all look the same.'

When she walked past them, she was mostly safe, because of her own name being 'Miranda'.

She would walk through the school halls, trying to avoid direct confrontation with their cult scouts, and would see them saying her own name, with their ever stary, creepy eyes. She guessed they hung about in halls, because they were cannibals.

It conveniently rhymed. She didn't suppose they were ashamed of their eating habits. Cannibals were not known for their ethics or morals, so they weren't intentionally hiding their sub-human life style by their hunting position. They were disguising their collective name from possible victims. Some might miss-hear rumours, and think it was 'am in the halls,' instead of 'cannibals'.

It was the same reason they behaved like animals. Animals,

rhymed with cannibals. With just eyes to talk with, the two words could easily become confused.

'That's Miranda' the mirror-spy would say to the other mirror-spies, with her eyes, and the crowd would part to let her through. 'Mirror- and –her' it looked like, as if they were on intimate terms. 'We are with her already,' it implied.

She detested them but they couldn't see it. Self-love was a well known feature of cults. They couldn't see their own faults. If one Mirror was made a judge, and the other Mirror was a mass murdering criminal, the mass murderer would be found innocent. Miranda sighed into her duvet. She had sprawled all morning. Bed sprawling was a way of getting out of making the bed. Making the bed wasn't a hard task. She only had a duvet and sheet to manoeuvre or change, so she put it off for something to do when she was feeling simple minded. She was never simple minded, so the bed never got made. Magazines and crumpled newspaper pages fell from the bed as she turned. Some of the newspaper pages were shaped and ironed by her sleeping weight. The sheets had a slight blue tinge, from when she had un - expectedly dozed, while still wearing her jeans.
She stared at the ceiling, a blank expression on her features. It was a practised, non committal look that she had spent years perfecting. She didn't want wrinkles when she was older.
She didn't want her grand parents knowing what she was thinking either.
And if she made a facial movement at school, she might be pounced on.

Miranda unset her face to remind her that she was in her own bedroom, and not in the canni-halls, and swung her body round. She did yoga upside down. It was more effective for her, than the usual sitting position, but only when it was facial yoga.

She could also check under the bed for tell tale signs of hurried occupation. Some strange people out there may try and live in her house, when she was out. Some doubles were like that. They hunted on their own. They were called Cook-you's. They chucked the person out of their own homes, but not until they had convinced others it was their own. They called themselves, with their eyes only, 'daughters', which of course was 'stalkers', of the house.

She was meant to be meeting Graham, but she didn't feel like meeting him, now that she had thought about it.

Myra, Myra,
In the hall,
You are standing next to a
Cannibal.

Myra, Myra
Now you've grown so tall
Your boyfriend might
 be the same…..fool.

She changed yoga position again, by sticking her tongue out at the wall opposite.

Witches and Switches. Did they really think that she had been fooled by one letter difference?

She had been safe so far, since she was born, but had seen the way the witches she had lived with looked at her, and the mirror. She didn't know if they were just getting used to her name again, or if they were practising meeting themselves, as they gazed at it. She had also seen Eileen studying the back of her own leg with such intensity she had thought she was going to go out to ambush another, unlike-her, face. One she had only seen from behind, in a skirt.

And the nearest supermarket was only five minutes away.

Miranda had stopped eating home made pies, when she was old enough to reach the fridge handle herself. Better safe than sorry, she thought.

Graham had been warned against being a Switch, the same as she had. The Switches lives, they had been told, were an endless round of copy cat, where they played pass-the-parcel with other people's addresses, while working for employment agencies. They were pushed into, or persuaded, to be Switches by the cults, who promised the unbelievable if they did the immoral or illegal.

Witches were a different sort of unbelievable.
They would make spells, wishes and curses, spend four nights singing to the moon, go skinny dipping in a reddened lake and buy soft metal pendants to swing, in the belief that doing all that made the phone bill appear exactly a week after all the indoctrinations, when the phone bill always appeared at that time of the month, on that day, at that time.
Why bother witching, when the result would be the same? It was all so childish.

Arthur liked the word 'Whirl- lough' [waerlock] better than witch. It was less immature and more fireproof. He was a one man campaign against centre fires. A Whirl-lough was wind and water making an effort, without any help from anything else. They were elements combining themselves into a hurricane through the water. That was what real m'ag'tic was. Just the elements, said Arthur, making tics and the tics made the illnesses.

Miranda thought Arthur was a saddo too.
They all belonged in a role playing game.

43

Arthur looked at her cousins wrists too closely, for her liking. He was a bit strange.

Miranda stared at the ceiling, and felt her cheeks pull.

☼

Graham was sitting on a garden bench.

The garden bench was placed outside the converted village hall. The hall was a mini-cinema for local residents. Him and Miranda had been planning to see an old film. The film depended on the time of day. As it was morning, they were probably showing an old scary film. Scary films faded back into slight fears by night time. If it was night time, they would show a comedy, so cinema goers could sleep with a smile on their faces.

Miranda was late. She was normally late anyway, so he amused himself while watching other potential girlfriends walk by.

She, he thought, was a 'slib' rather than a 'slob'. Slobs tended not to want to do anything, so they didn't. Slibs didn't want to do anything, but eventually did. She was thinner. She had lost her 'o' shape.

The 'slib' had better hurry.

Graham was a year older than Miranda. One of his pet names for her was 'cotton bud.'

When her hair had been short, she looked like one.

Now it was long, the thick blonde curls stuck out everywhere.

He would hide his head in them. His head had always been in the clouds anyway.

Another pet name for her was 'cirrus.'

Sometimes he called her 'nimbus.' if she looked stormy enough.

He counted how many pet names he had for her, so he wouldn't feel too annoyed at her slibby lateness, before eventually pulling out his family book. They all had a copy. Years before they had a shared website, and had added to it all that they thought was wise and witty. On reflection it hadn't been, but it had bonded

44

the family together. When there had been an electrical storm causing a black out, they all said that it would be a shame if the situation had been permanent. They agreed that the one website they would miss, should the internet be wiped out, would be their own inane blogs, so decided to put them altogether in one book. They self published one hundred copies. Graham's copy was battered, and old. They had named the book, 'The book of words', because it was.

Graham had been thinking of going home, to his mother's house, and he subconsciously turned to an appropriate page.

'The Book of Words'
'Words can be very dangerous on the equilibrium of mental health.
Strangely, it is the word, 'Logic' and implications that can have a lasting disturbance on reasoning abilities, if looked at deeply.'
For example;
LOGIC; madness should be the direct opposite of sanity, but it is a question of your incomprehension of another's reality that makes another's reality insane... Their perception of your reality, in comparison, is also one of madness. So, madness would be seen as a two way mood, when it obviously isn't. This line of logical thinking can drive you to lunacy, as the more you question the particular nuances of mental illness, the more illogical the LOGIC is that drives you mad.
People suffering from this LOGICAL LUNACY were often recommended , by their doctors, to sit in a flowering garden, in the hope that the flowers philosophy of growth, with it's impeccable symmetrical, logical, mathematical form, will influence the sufferers, returning their brain to a more '1+1=2' way of thinking.
The more serious sufferers of LOGICAL LUNACY, the ones

that were mad, got the wrong end of the stem sometimes, and took garden staring to be a literal action. They are the ones that tended to brush themselves up and down little green plants, hoping some normality will stick to them. Some others looked at the greenery and said to themselves, 'that tree is me', in the same way they would a look-a-like human. They were mostly safe until they met an axe-wielding maniac. Axe-wielding maniacs are normally sane until they meet someone who insists they are a tree, and then they tended to have a bout of LOGICAL LUNACY. Also, those that stared at gardens for too long sometimes had an unreasonable amount of sympathy and pity for the plants. When tree sympathisers got an unreasonable urge of empathy, they tended to, when there was a fire about, start feeling sorry for the burning sticks, and tried to rescue them. (That's how fire juggling started.) They were also mistaken for angry mobs when they tried to return the burning sticks to the tree they come from, their 'mothers'. (Now door shaped pieces of wood.)

Graham's mother suffered the normal symptoms of mental anguish that could be classed as instability.

Graham used to say lack of understanding of others was the beginning of his mother's particular mental condition, but changed his mind when he got older, after studying biology at school. After studying it, he started to say 'the $98*x$ $h19$ in her serotonin level has been affected by $rs35j$ compound that emanates from her left shin.'

Through her worse moments of deliriums, he'd add, 'oh no, someone's made off with the $f19dx$ and the $ugt6x$ as well. No dinner tonight then.' before escaping as fast as he could to the peaceful quietness of the fields behind the house. Sometimes he'd buy her a brown shoelace on the way home, to help her regain her balance.

46

'The book of Words.' also mentions this about madness;

'Dea (th) je vue' is when you know something hideous has happened before and is happening again, but you can't remember what happens next in the sequence because it was either too shocking or horrific to remember. This is seen as tragic, as obviously, if you can't remember the next event, you can't avoid it, so therefore it will happen again and you won't be able to remember it again. No one knows what could be that horrific, unless it was death, and it couldn't have been your own death, as you wouldn't be alive, so it is called 'death je vue' which of course is someone else's death that you have been told about or warned about, which could be yours as well, as you look the same. D' je vue can be avoided by not doing the same as the recently deceased 'you' – an example of not doing the same is not to go door knocking, take drugs or try to rob someone while carrying a potential lethal weapon. Also don't believe people who tell you they have a room free for you to live in, recently vacated by your look-a-like. They are probably the murderers.'

'Adult'er me' is the oddest and most normal revelation. It is when you remember the exact moment you decided who you disliked intensely and never wanted to grow up like, followed by an honest glimpse at your own personality and the peculiar likeness you have to the person you disliked intensely. This is followed by the probable future you would have if you continued being like that person. (Helped by your memory of the disliked person's life.) It is very depressing and seems more like a revelation of your future than the statistical probability that it is.
'Adult 'er - e' is more likely to happen near Christmas time, with the broadcasting of Scrooge, as it is a very cheap DIY version of the same story and because some people can be so

easily influenced that they can have an episode of Scrooge just by looking at a bag of crisps. (The half-word association is enough for them. 'Crisps', to some people, is near enough to the word 'Christmas' to bring on a bout of self-doubt and self loathing, without any particular insight to their own lifestyle. Do not buy such people a multi-pack of Sainsbury's own brand as this may bring on a bad episode of lunacy.) D'je vue is sometimes linked to Adult'er'e.

And this is also what is written about MADNESS, SWITCHES,
 Lesser (lower) switches used repetitive gesturing and looks to hypnotise people into believe they were hearing words that weren't being spoken, blinding the eyes with mime and time, inducing SCHISOPHRENIA. Mostly only the same Switches looked at each other long enough for this to happen, but it can happen to Innocents. Innocents are people who have kept their heads bent down all their life, then suddenly look up and notice other people. This normally happens to catering staff, littler pickers and factory workers, but only for a short acclimatising period. Sometimes school children suffer with this too as they are normally eager for knowledge and interests so try to translate looks into words, without realising it. It is best for school children and babies to ignore eye- talkers , for their own mental health, and to make sure they verbally communicate.
If you think it's someone else you can hear, but they didn't say the words, they implied them, it's best to talk to yourself to try and understand those implications, and to absolve guilt if none of the actions implied were yours.
TV schizophrenia is more common and a hundred times more annoying because it really does a lot of implying and persuading. Try to remember it basically is all about the weather, and the TV doesn't know anyone personally.

MADNESS AND PROFITEERING.

When confusion and shock happens to a large crowd there are always Switches trying to making a profit through shock induced purchasing. It is thought that word-association, and the same type of Switch miming, is used as a catalyst before a crowd is hysterical. CHOC was named to rhyme with SHOCK. To avoid the SHOCK people will probably, instantly, reach for the CHOC instead, hoping to by-pass any SHOCKING scenes.

This is wide scale object Switching. It is a pre planned psychological attack on the senses, meant to take advantage of chaos. The army and police used to deal with this kind of wide-scale Switching by giving away free sweeties, while wearing furry fancy-dress costumes, hoping that the Switches wouldn't make a profit from inducing fear.

Don't reach for CROC instead of CHOC. It is a bad idea and will only induce more SHOCK, which will make you reach for more CROC or choc. Croc reaching is a never ending circle until one bites your arm off. Always eat food off crockery to avoid spontaneous arm loss due to unconscious CROCADILE reaching.

Years ago the same fancy dressed police would deal with severe hypnotising Switches by covering them with a large sheet of black cloth so their meaningful gestures and faces couldn't be seen.

Even though they started to believe they were electrical boxes, due to their appearance and general shape, they had to verbalise their communication, rather than act it out.

Repetitive verses stopped them from weighing words with unintentional meaning, and they were showed, quite

graphically, what the church used to do to Switches to stop them behaving in another over-influencing way, in the form of a statue of a man tied to a cross, (to keep their hands still).

Graham shut the book, and went home.

He was tired of waiting.

Henry and Arthur left the pub, after the distracting and hypnotic clouds had caught the Switches attention.
They walked in silence, for a little while.
They usually did after seeing the angel cloud. It *was* very disturbing, in a nice way. When they were children they used to run after it, but made sure they were distracted straight afterwards, so they didn't have to think about where it came from much. The few minutes' silence they shared back then became a habit.

Arthur broke the silence. He felt that he ought to remind Henry that Miranda might be better behaved when she was a bit older. Most people were.
'Do you remember a girl called Rene who came to stay with me a while back?' Arthur said after a few moments.
Henry shook his head. 'Can't say I do Arthur. Has she any relevance to genetic growth behaviour?'
'What? I can't say that she has, Henry. Also she is totally unrelated to the catering side of the chemistry or science industry. What I was going to say is that she is arriving today to visit again. For a bit longer. She's a university girl now, so maybe I am wrong, and she is. She wants to save a bit of money, so I'm letting her work in the shop. She's at the house now.

50

Miranda will be off to college soon too, won't she? Now I remember what I was going to say. The clouds, Henry. Do you know how long I have watched the clouds? For years. And in all my years of cloud watching I have noticed that the clouds come in all shapes and forms. They are mostly in the shape of faces and animals, yes, but, and this makes me believe you are wrong about mesosphere influence; they are strangely prudent. There are no Breasts, Henry. No breasts, Vaginas, or Penises are up there with the rest of the impression of humanity. Not distinct images, like that face is. I say to you that humanity is a bit older than what the clouds have become. I would add that those clouds were made by Virgin.com or British Telecom, and not by a conscious mass of atomic gases. Wouldn't you? Virgins are well known for not showing their own genitals, so I would say it was Virgin, but the BBC also have connotations connected to their name too....'

 Henry nodded, wondering why he had never noticed the lack of sexual organs in cloud formations before. Arthur was right. They were the only indistinct forms in clouds of certainties.

Miranda looked at her mobile and sighed. He never phoned her when she was late, either. She had never had that negative excitement of an unexpected call. She finished her jowl exercises before standing up, and putting her coat on. If she left now she would be ale to avoid Eileen, and walk behind the ghoul houses. The ghoul houses were empty-part buildings, and most people avoided the footpath that run behind them. They had been left as derelict buildings because of the bizarre idea of the former owner, who thought he would be wealthier if he rid the house of nice tenants, and filled it with convicts instead. The convicts would then murder the next door neighbours, so he could buy the property cheaper – no one wanted to buy slaughter, stalker houses- and then he would be twice as rich.

The owner was murdered instead, and the convicts were arrested. They had had the same idea as the landlord, but thought of him first.

The rumour that they had sold both, and had emigrated, wasn't persuasive, as the houses had been half knocked down afterwards to stop the same sort of people moving in.

Graham had left the park bench, but Graham was still there.

Miranda had been right about Graham being a Switch, but he wasn't aware of it himself. He was a victim of a Switch. He had been followed.

Graham had been followed before, but most people were. For most people, leaving the house was like walking through a well known danger zone. The world was filled with stalkers. Most of the people were opportunists, and looked so obviously normal that they made their intentions clear. A few streets, away from Graham's, was normally a man who spent days walking up and down with a letter to post. He never actually posted it, but to someone who was casually looking, he didn't seem to be loitering.

Graham's stalker was named Graham too. He had been named Graham by a money-mad woman who thought she could take the place of any other mother of a Graham. She was very stupid. People like her saw no difference between people or objects. The only time that she had been right about objects is when she practised hand to eye coordination with a shape sorter. She thought people were the same test, and had got annoyed at passing people when they showed independent thought.

Her Graham looked the same as Graham, and that was enough for her. It should be enough for anyone else.

Her Graham wasn't amusing himself by stomping by the side of the cinema, after Graham had left. He was quite patient, and careful, with his stomping. His pacing was hidden from the high street by a few trees. He had seen Graham walk away, and his mother had nagged him out of the car to see whether he had left anything useful at the park bench.

Her Graham didn't like stalking, but he was too young to move out of his mother's house. He stomped, in case the slightly older Graham had left anything dropped on the grass. He didn't want to pick it up, as if he was an old fashioned psychopathic tramp, collecting everything he could about his victim. He felt the earth compact under his feet, and felt as if he had made a move towards his own independence. Smiling, he went to walk back to the car, empty handed.

Miranda always attracted his attention first. She had stopped him a few times, mistaking him for Graham. He hadn't told her he wasn't, but had looked carefully past her, into shop windows, to see if his reflection was that similar. He had never seen Graham with the same intimacy as Miranda had. He didn't think they looked exactly alike.

He hadn't noticed her approaching.

'C'mon.' She smiled at him.

'What?' Her Graham tried not to show his confusion. His mother, just visible from where he was standing, waved at him, pleased, and drove off.

'Are you annoyed at me, for being late? The film probably hasn't started yet.'

Her Graham shook his head. 'Of course not….Yes. ..Lets.'

Her Graham didn't want to. He would wait until he could sneak away, and go as quickly as possible. He could have all day, to himself, without his nagging mother to question him.

Mrs. Lock stared at Miranda. Miranda didn't recognise her and she shouldn't have. Mrs. Lock had only seen Miranda as she had passed her in the street.

Mrs. Lock was an old Switch, but she had stopped switching a long time ago. The village was her home now. Being a Switch had made her wiser, if lonelier. She hardly let anyone near her now, but she was good at remembering faces.

Miranda had just mistaken that man for her boyfriend, when he had just climbed out of a car. Mrs. Lock turned back on the path. 'Oi , Miranda. That isn't Graham. Graham got fed up of waiting, and went home.' She knew everyone's name. They told her it as she walked past, if she raised her head, with their eyes. She had to raise her head occasionally, to see where she was going. She couldn't leave Miranda to that Graham, when she had just passed Graham.

Her Graham stared at Mrs. Lock's wrinkled face.
Miranda looked from one to the other.
'What's she saying, Graham?'
Her Graham looked at the space his mother car had been in.

Mrs. Lock tugged on Miranda's arm. He was too tall to argue with. Taller than Miranda's Graham.
'You seeing a film, you say? What's on?' She said to Miranda, intervening.
Miranda looked at her blankly. 'What?' she snarled. 'Look for yourself.' She added.
Graham was walking away, with a large stride. She wasn't the type to run after him.

'I saw your Graham go home. Then that one got out of a car. I think. There might be more of them. They could kill me for what I just said to you. Let's go inside the cinema; somewhere safe.'
Miranda stared at the old woman's aged hand in disgust. As her

arm had risen to meet with her own, the smell of body odour had wafted off her, making Miranda feel sick.

She gagged slightly but nodded her head.

Mrs. Lock added, in a slightly more pathetic way, 'I was a relief assistant teacher at your junior school, if you are trying to place my face. That's how I know your name,' she lied, and held her wrist tighter. She shuffled to the cinema door, dragging her with her. 'You'll have to pay. I haven't got any money.'

Miranda nodded, silently. She couldn't understand why Graham had just walked off. She couldn't understand that he really *was* a Switch.

She pointed to the board randomly, and despondently. 'Two tickets to that.' She said to the caretaker.

Mrs. Lock hid her smile. She hadn't seen a film in ages, and after the film had finished she'd take Miranda to a café and let her explain herself. She looked like the type to fill in the gaps; mouthy, and glad to hear her own voice. The type to allow little old women pull her about, too satisfied with her own strength to feel threatened.

The village hall had been converted in to a cinema eons ago. The wall were thick enough to withstand the weather, and it was also on Big House land, so it still had electricity from the Big House generator whenever the village power lines went out.

It was a small and broken building. A large old oak tree had fallen on it, back in the nineteen hundreds. The tree was left in its fallen-over-position, as there were no lumberjacks around to move it. The end wall was rebuilt on the other side of it, shrinking the village hall dimensions by a third. Those who couldn't afford to go to the cinema would walk the length of the fallen tree, sit on the top and get a view of the bottom half of the screen through the small, hastily made stained-glass type window. Bottle plastic was cheaper than stained glass and the village had made its own window from green, transparent and orange plastic bottles. The window was a bit bowed, in places, and the figure of St.Mary's dress smelt of cider, but it was a very good amateur attempt. There was on old extended archway, where church notices were pinned. The church notices were so old that one read 'church fund now at '10 shillings and thrupence.' Underneath some one had added 'now at ten pounds,' followed by, 'Now at £1000000, 0000 and they still haven't replaced the toilet seat cover.' Other notices read 'aerobics to the latest film. 7.00pm. Tuesday- no under 12's allowed.' And the eternal, 'for sale-Bread bin and cheese board-pine, unused gift.' Graham was saving up for that one. His mother, in a fit of annoyance, had bought that cheese board when he was ten years old. He had been showing off his reading talents to her, while waiting for the early Saturday cinema to begin. Unknowingly to him, the notice had already been there for two years previously.

And the notice was still there after she had bought them.

Graham was saving the money, so he could buy the next ten year's worth of pine bread bins and cheese boards in advance. Then there would be no pine bread and cheese board sign to annoy his mother. The problem was, he had, pondered, what would he do with all the pine? Would he succumb to the 'for sale.' poster habit? No, he was going to build a path with the cheese boards and bird houses with the bread bins.

At the other side of the cinema was the graveyard. From the graveyard there was a view to the hill with the willow tree on it. It was the willow tree mentioned in Graham's book so he decided to climb the hill instead of going home. He could check that no one was tied up underneath it.

'Willow tree nr see-you-bought-a-comb river;

It used to be fashionable to carry a long stick; a 'will know' stick, if you liked to walk. It was usually inscribed with the names of towns and maps on it to save the traveller walking around in circles. As it was decorated with maps it was a useful guide to where people come from too. It was also known as a 'wand' (short for 'wandering stick') .

It became usual to have an engraving, a sign, or a drawing, indicating the village the traveller originated from. This meant if the traveller fell ill or worse, they could be taken home.

It became so usual that when a traveller with no engraved stick appeared he was thought to be a beggar and a tramp. He or she would be greeted though, and made to feel welcome. If he boasted of evil doings, or hinted towards the worst sins, he would be helped to a willow tree on the pretence of finding a stick. He or she would be chained to the tree, once there; the hanging leaves would be quickly plaited, (See; maypole dancing, local origin of ;) and the branches nailed into the ground. On a still day, no-one would notice the lack of movement of the tree, but on a windy day the stillness of the leaves would hint at what it was used for.

If the stranger was honest and good then they would be sent to a willow tree for a stick, which would be engraved with directions for the next town or village.

Now of course, visitors have USB memory sticks. These are sometimes scratched with the same old patterns and markings as a 'will know' stick. If you ever meet someone with a USB memory stick that is similar to a 'will know' stick and has scratched maps on the SURFACE, rather than it being loaded with maps, then avoid them. They are obviously thick.

The ground around the willow was undisturbed when he reached it, and he relaxed by the foot of the tree, while deciding what to do next.

Chapter 3

'**The pyramids were built by people who did upside down yoga in attics.**
It is imagined the artist was upside down in a dining chair while she did the drawings of the attic and put herself in the diagram as a taxable wall decoration while testing herself for spatial abilities, and while marking how many rats and pigeons were on the window sills. The real pyramid architectural drawings – the ones where the buildings were to be made from steel and glass that sparkled in the sun and sand were presumably swapped for the attic drawings in the hope that there was money to be embezzled if they were built in the style of the attic, and in concrete. You could tell by looking at the pyramids that the attic artist was also wondering where the chimney had disappeared to, whether there would be room for an en suite shower room and where the cat had gone.'

Graham did yoga, so he understood. Miranda had taught him. He did it upside down and spent hours trying to turn his straight beard growth into curly beard growth, and to get his muscles to grow, while sketching and thinking of ways to make money. He was teaching his beard to obey the law of gravity. Curly beards were rare now-a-days. He would be different, and safer for a bit longer, from the mirrors of his world, if he cultivated a ringlet or two. The mummy was presumably stray thoughts about how the architect would look if she didn't exercise, or if she fell onto the ceiling.
Graham flicked forward a couple of pages.

'Cell phones are so sad. Not the object itself but the rumours of it.

When the next door neighbours listened through the wall, and heard uncle Whenter was a cell phone programmer, the rumour of it started all sorts of trouble. One mother said she sold cells too, and started trying to sell her cotton-bud saliva to the postman. She had never 'managed to program cells' she told him, while waving a bud at him; 'the family down the road had managed, but no matter how many times she had tried commanding her own skin to do things, it never worked for her.' She thought the blood cells had their own genetic thing going on, and didn't need programming, she had added, but 'if that's what Mrs. Blue scarf said cell programming meant, she would give it a try'.

The family down the road had been at it for years, so she didn't know what was so special about it. Their skin cells were programmed with all sorts of images. Honestly.

This rumour of how people were being paid for cell programming was spread until the chemist run out of cotton-buds, and until the newspapers picked the story up. The newspaper decided to point people to the relevant web pages, on the internet, and that was the end of the misunderstanding.

Then the phone's name was changed to a 'mobile phone' instead.

After a few flurries of phone throwing, not a lot happened with that name.

There was one local incident where the local supermarket manager tried to train the shoppers – he said they were his 'mob' – by using a flow chart diagram, a loud speaker, and the shops alarms, so he could get a job as the same mobile programmer, but that was all. He also tried to turn the

60

television over while driving so everyone discounted him as a nutter.

Graham had sort of remembered all that from when he was a child. The local gossips hadn't let the rumour die a natural old age, but had kept bringing it alive again. He still got accosted by the 'GO TO' line, who was still claiming to be the now very dead manager's children. The children had mistaken being 'biped, cold', as being 'binary code'. He could tell. They walked around wearing short T-Shirts, in the middle of winter, while trying to make people go where they didn't want to go. There was also the long dead manager's wife impersonators, who thought they were the 'IF' line, and who suddenly started to believe in 'equal rights', thinking it was the same as '= >'.
They kept appearing by the supermarket back door, wanting a lift home, unconcerned that they were obviously not the manager's wife and that the couple were long dead [due to old age]. When the lift didn't appear they would have a change of personality and think they were singular again. Then they would run around, arms outstretched, saying 'we free' instead. The words were similar enough for them, and they looked like they were catching airwaves. Sometimes they dressed as pagans, and sometimes as May-day princesses.

He remembered his dad saying that there also used to be a lot of self-learn-while-you-are-asleep tapes around, and everyone thought that the whole managerial family had tried to learn basic programming while snoring.
He also remembered his dad saying that the riots had started when the Microsoft windows program had kept crashing. Windows all over the country started to be broken. Especially chip shops. They for some reason, in the world of dreams, chip shops turned into IP addresses.
That learn-while-you sleep tape was lethal.

Graham looked around, and down the hill. He thought that, on the way up, he had seen Miranda, but couldn't be sure. He was so lucky that she had been unaffected by computer engineering. She could still talk without a prompt line.

Graham shut the book. It would be funny if it hadn't been true.

Corrupted hard drives used to sometimes result in car crashes, by people who thought they were corrupted. Bad memory storage produced a few forgetful criminals, or people who could only remember things if they were in bed.

He stood up, and slowly started walking home.

Mrs Lock watched the film silently. She had seen it before. She began to doze.

Graham had noticed her loitering about when he walked through the small High street. He had called her Flow Chart, the sad beggar woman, she thought.

Mrs Lock was scared of the other Switches, especially those that didn't talk. When they are in a position where talking is unavoidable, they would 'bark' their words out in a domineering and aggressive way, as if they are about to bite. She didn't like that.

She had been part of a loosely connected bunch of Switches, when she had been one. They did not swap homes or jobs, but swapped… erm.. acting roles… and..er… occupations. One week she had been a shop lifter, the next a con-woman. She wasn't a murderer; she didn't steal identities or babies and was a vegetarian. She remembered where she saw Miranda and her grandmother. It was in a vegetarian shop, picking up some soya products.

No, she wasn't one of those 'Proud to be an animal' types, like some of the Switches were. No quadruped lifestyle for her. She liked her own two feet and she didn't want her toes to be divided into two sets of hoofs, to match her palm print. She knew that's why they also they wore witches hats and sought each other out, so there was two of them. Two of those hat shapes made the same hoof print that were in her hand. They felt they had met the other half of their body when they met her, while she felt as if she would be holding the hand of a pig when she met them.

The Switches were hand obsessed.

Perhaps it was because they thought they didn't have any. She had never actually seen them use their hands to *do* anything.

She was more of a humanitarian Switch, if she was a Switch at all. Not a robbing the good type of person. She tried to persuade people not to do bad things. She would follow curses around and try and persuade the people that they were wishes instead. This was done by silently, slowly, changing the words of the curse, with rhyming looks. This was about the only time she was silent though.

Miranda stared at the screen.

She wasn't that naïve to believe that this was a real life situation.

She had been witched.

She had never been witched before.

She fumed inwardly.

Any moment now it would wear off – the mind numbing brain-washing would.

The strange fat woman with the alternative perfume would disappear as quickly as she had appeared.

All she had to do was wait.

She closed her eyes. She had heard about witchful thinking. Hers had been to have normal parenting. She had trained herself to respond to helpless old–aged pensioners, probably, and in a moment of shock, had made the wrong decision. She wouldn't do it again. This old woman put her right off having an alternative granny of her own.

☼

England is a small island compared to the rest of the world. Even when it wasn't compared it was pretty small, so everything was mingled. Everyone knew about everyone, eventually. Spying on others is ethically, lawfully, and morally wrong. Also it wasn't needed, in a place so small, but some still did. They searched personal belongings and in houses, hoping to find something that didn't remind them of what they were themselves. Some just listened at walls. Strangely, wall-listeners were sometimes more persecuted than in-house robbers perhaps because the wall-listeners would think up nonsense excuses about why they were doing what they were doing, and that could be very annoying to people who weren't interested. One common nonsense excuse was that they were influenced by the map of Great Britian, and being like a giant ear. They thought it looked like an ear, anyway.

They were supposed to listen in on what others were saying, they said, because they were ear-lets. [People Born of The Ear; Earls when they grow up, or, in the more modern context, URLs.]

The coven cult-leader Switch, who had been talking to herself, would have heard about the possible Miranda Switch, and the cloud forming, just above the cloud angel, eventually, just by sitting around on a bus or by going shopping, but receiving text messages about the lifestyle of people she didn't know made her feel less like a tramp, gathering rubbish to examine, and more like she was liked. Lots of text messages meant she could lean her head to one side too and show people her long neck. She was proud of her long neck.

'What an idiot; after all these years; You would have thought they would have learnt their lesson, but maybe they had just forgotten.' She had blurted out to the driving wheel, on the way to the village, as if she was burping. She had raised a hand to her mouth, in remembered manners, and turned on her mobile phone. She may need to start recording her mouth, if blurting was going to be a regular event. It had been her fault. She had forgotten to adjust her side mirror, and had caught sight of her own head again, instead of the road behind. She was so easily swayed by her own beauty, she thought, smiling.

Self-delusion is a tool to be used to influence others she had been taught, and she smiled at herself at any chance she got. It only seemed to work with her own twin likeness though. They believed they were beautiful too.

Mrs. Lock and Miranda looked at each other.

After the film had finished Miranda had tried to get away, but the old woman had said that she could tell her more about 'mothered Graham', and that her leg was hurting.

Now they were sitting in the only restaurant in the village, staring at the bread rolls in the middle of the table. The restaurant wasn't old, or a restaurant, but a café that converted itself. Old places had bread rolls in the centre of the tables. Not now. Not in this century, but the owner worked at the bread factory and bought them home with him, in a sad and generous way, in memory of the last century. He also thought that having bread rolls in the middle of the table would let everyone know he knows about local history, and that he knows about the dead that owned the café before he did. He was actions, not words, in communication and deed.

Bread roll = dead, know. He knew it didn't really rhyme, but just a hint of rhyming might gently let everyone know, that he knows.

He got tired of people telling him about others dying, that they were more acquainted with the dead than him, and decided that he would let them slowly figure it out themselves, why he feeds the beggar that spies on funerals.

He recognised the beggar, and Miranda he had seen from a distance. He put the bread rolls in the middle, just for the beggar woman, before she started to tell him that she knew his double was already dead....

'Lucky I turned up, else, or anything may have happened'. Mrs. Lock grinned.

Miranda looked at her sullenly before replying; 'right. Thanks for letting me know...so, you have seen him before...?'

'Only a few times. He is careful, that one. His mum's a pushy cow. ...He is from the derth hills ...'

Miranda raised her eye brows. ' dirth hills?'

'Dirth hills. Devil's . From the Death hills. Deaf hills, then, if you want to pick on my accent. .. You know.. the Ear that Cannot Hear...The Baby that Is Never Born, the Fairy that Never Flies, the Nose that Never Smells, the Dog that Is Always on Two Feet... are you sure you was born around here?'

Miranda stared at her 'You mean Ireland? No one has spoken like that for years. So he is Irish?'

'No.' Mrs Lock looked around the café. She knew Miranda's mum called herself a Witch. Witches were untouchable in the Switch world. There was no point in Switching with a Witch, because every one knew they were evil. Swapping with one of those was like saying you were the psycho with the knife, all along. It was like recognising yourself on a wanted poster, *and* admitting it was you. Your own face would never forgive you for saying that.

Mrs. Lock has seen Miranda's mum about for years. She was a weird one too. Mrs. Lock was pretty certain that unwanted Switches were sent to the witch's house, just so they got killed, then replaced. It kept their world moving.

'He is from the Dirth hill -deaf hi'll, devils. They have spied on your Graham. Or his mum has. I have seen the way she bullies him. I wouldn't be surprised if he had been a stolen baby. They are like that. I 'm not. Uck.'

Whether to tell Miranda what she thought about her mother was another thing. She would wait until she had something to eat and drink first. She had never been to the restaurant before. Deaf and ill - mentally, she would have added, in case Miranda still hadn't understood what she meant by dearth hills, which was a place as well as a noun, but she didn't feel like explaining every turn her slang language moved. Miranda should know herself by now what local phrases meant.

The café was only a restaurant at night time. The owner changed the name of it when the sun set. He had a roller sign where the normal painted sign normally went, above the shop, which turned.

He avoided tax, and Switches, by turning the sign round. He was even thinking of quartering the sign, and changing the back into to a book shop, with an art supply shop upstairs. He would have two entrances, and just close one, to confuse his enemies.

Villages had a low profit margin, so he barely had a living from the restaurant / café itself. The job at the bread making factory helped, but he had forgot to turn the roller around after closing the night before. He still had the restaurant's name up, and the same table cloths. They were reversible.

Miranda frowned, 'Are you trying to sound ominous?'

'No! I am trying to tell you that is what they do. Besides you are a bit big to be a kidnapped baby aren't you? I am hardly going to fit you in my bag. It is only a shoulder bag, not a shopping trolley. I suppose I could pop home and get it. Then you could stand in it and I could wheel you away. If that's your fantasy, then you'll have to pay. But I want you to know, that I know, *that* depiction is another part of the map; Norway and Ireland. I know, I know, so don't tell me. I am just saying. It was the way I was taught to talk.'

Mrs. Lock grabbed a roll from the basket and offered it to Miranda. 'You are a bit skinny so you'd fit.'

Miranda stared at her. She had never heard so many words, given freely, in such a short space of time. She was beginning to enjoy herself. Throughout the film she had been over powered by Mrs. Lock's lack of hygiene. She had not been really taking notice of her though. Old people didn't interest her. She didn't take any notice of Henry and Arthur either. Mrs. Lock talked like they did, but wasn't her relative. That is why she was interesting.

She had been thinking of Graham's betrayal. He must have known.

Miranda smiled and took the bread roll. 'You wouldn't.'

Mrs. Lock wasn't laughing. The girl was obviously mistreated. Her bones were sticking out everywhere on her face. It matched her hair, which was blonde bone shaped curls. Perhaps she was trying to camouflage her face as hair too.

She was glad she had never lived with witches and she decided not to mention Miranda's living conditions, or her relatives, until Miranda did, or else Miranda would think that Mrs. Lock knew all about her.

Living with the witches must be bad. She had heard how they fattened their children up until they were ready to cook them; nasty people.

Mrs. Lock always thought it wasn't their own children but the Switches. How else would they be able to move families away from their own home? She thought they probably stole their children first, then gave the ones that wanted to go back home for the witches to eat. Miranda looked as if she had witnessed this, and had refused the same fattening.

68

Miranda, nibbling at the roll, looked at Mrs. Lock. There was something… she stopped eating and stared again.

Mrs. Lock's eyes had just changed colour, and her cheeks had thinned out, giving her face a starving skinny look. Her brown eyes had just turned green.

Miranda held the bread roll out to her, curiously.

'No, thank you,' Mrs. Lock replied. Her eyes changed colour again, and her cheeks filled. Her eyes were now blue. Then images appeared on her face.

Miranda leaned back. This was astounding. Amazing. Miranda had never seen anything like it before. The outlines of the images formed as if Mrs. Lock had fallen asleep with her head on a crumbled, lumpy pillow. The lines were that deep and noticeable, but the images weren't sharp triangles, but gentle drawings. She was a Changeling. Miranda wanted to giggle. An old bag lady had just stepped out of a children's book. She didn't want to look away. She would have to keep Mrs. Lock talking.

'But you are staying to eat? I will pay.'

Mrs. Lock narrowed her eyes. Miranda looked too enthusiastic. It reminded her of… some one….she couldn't think… of a different time and place. She had, back then, just walked away. She had picked up her coat, and shut the door behind her. And had started walking….and walking….and walking.

Miranda leaned forward.

Mrs. Locks face now had a multitude of images, appearing on her skin. They looked distinct and real. Miranda reached forward, her hand ready to make contact with Mrs. Lock's cheek.

Mrs. Lock sneered and pulled her head back. That is what *they* used to do. 'What do you think you are doing?'

Miranda jumped back, and reddened. She was genuinely surprised at her own actions.

'I am so sorry. I thought I saw something on your face. What is it?'

Mrs. Lock was relieved. She had thought Miranda was a Switch herself for a moment or too. She didn't know what was on her face. She would get her pocket mirror and find out.

Miranda watched again as Mrs. Lock pulled a pocket mirror out of her pocket.
Mrs Lock's face become noticeably thinner, just before she looked in to the mirror. The images disappeared too, leaving Mrs. Locks face clear, but skinny. 'What is it? I can't see what you are talking about.'
'It fell off' Miranda replied quickly 'Now shall I buy us a salad?'

Rene let herself into Arthur's house. She was dressed in clothing too much like another's style- a long white skirt, with buttons down the front, grey shoes, and a flowery green blouse.
Far too old fashioned for her, but her mother had wanted her to self-curse a vain middle-aged woman who lived in the same village. She had dropped Rene there so they could bond. Rene thought her mum was being a bit of a loser, but weren't they all?
Rene checked the time. It had been two and a half hours since she had met the woman: time enough. She kicked off the brown brogues, and slipped them in the shoe rack. She stepped out of her skirt on the way up the stairs. She pulled the blouse over her head. Stopping at the bathroom, she washed the rather staid make up off, and spiked her hair with water. The vain woman had been dressed much the same as she had been.
Mirror, Mirror, on your own,
Call yourself same age grown.
Take her looks, one at a time,
And because you are herself
you will start to mime.

Some Switches never seem to learn. Mimicking isn't necessarily flattery. They can just be too vain.

Rene went back downstairs and looked around. The Switch that had followed her would have got tired of waiting outside. And he hadn't knocked on the door to find out if she was inside, so he had probably gone. Their excuse for stalking was normally a cat, which they bought with them. Cat-keeping had a double use. The stalker could let the cat go, and pretend to look for it as they searched for faces at windows and for unlocked doors. They could also look in the undergrowth for vegetables they planted the year before.

The one way to get rid of a stalker was for the householder to adopt the prowling cat, and train it not to go in the undergrowth.

Arthur had two or three cats that never went out. Rene had a quick look. No cats outside to rescue.

Rene grabbed her rucksack from the hall, and made her way back upstairs. She didn't like being a Switch and she hadn't been yet. She was waiting for her degree, to get a decent job. She would probably take someone else's job, while the someone else went on a well earned break. Arthur and her mum didn't know her plans. Her mum didn't mind her being a bit persuasive – that is what she called dressing in similar clothes, and visiting older people. She didn't care if Rene got murdered, or attacked, doing things like that for her, but didn't want her to swap lives with someone else, so Rene didn't tell her.

With the Switch she had just visited, she had used subtle eye movements. That one would persuade the woman that whatever Rene was telling her, she had thought of it herself.

Talking about history with her helped. Rene's own ideas would be in her past already and accepted.

Her mother had taught her that.

Her mother probably had cursed her too though, when she was asleep. That was the sort of thing Rene had witnessed her doing.

She thought her own mother wasn't very nice.

When she was a baby she had to cling. When she was older she knew she had been cursed herself because she kept going home. She was still clinging on, like an overgrown doll, to someone she didn't like.

She had noticed her mother talking to the other children when they were asleep. It was fairy tales, at first, and then it was a set of instructions of what she would like for Mother's day.

Mixing 'Once upon a time there was', 'a bottle of perfume' just didn't work though.

Switches are well known for their horrible nasty voices when they are within earshot, and are the talkative type - you have to pay them to talk in a normal way - but they do use their sweeter voices for free, when you are asleep. Perhaps that is where her mother had gone wrong. She always used her normal voice.

Switches thought it made a difference.

Graham would, and did say, the screeching switches were computer tape deck casualties too. He named them Tape Decks. He imagined that they had also listened to the how-to tape of computing, while they were asleep. He had imagined it thrown away, picked up, thrown away, sold at a jumble sale, thrown away, then sold again at a charity shop…It had legendary bread bin status for him.

The Tape Decks thought they controlled movement, because as soon as they started screeching people would move away. Graham avoided the Tape Decks. They reminded him of old skin-colour- prejudiced horror movies, with the blue eyed people getting attacked by chunks of blackness. If he heard that screech now, in the middle of the night, he would shut the double glazed windows to block out the noise.

Rene kept a door-stop for her college door, but was quite easy about talking to others when they were asleep, to get her own way. Some were gullible, some were not.

In her town the Tape Decks were called 'Birds' that made human

'Herds'. It was a name they called themselves. They were 'heard about twitter' but had never heard of a computer. They 'twittered' outside, in gangs, and when there was no answering bird call, they screeched like trapped birds. She avoided the gangs of birds, and tried to get the bus everywhere.

Her room at Arthur's was clean and spacious, even if it was a bit old fashioned. The carpet was a light pink and the bedspread white, with large pink flowers. A few vases of flowers were spotted around the room. In fact, they were more like bouquets. One of the advantages of owning a flower shop, she supposed.

She threw her rucksack down and unpacked. It was so good to be away from all that. It was so quiet. And every thing smelt so good.

Arthur had left a note and the shop keys. No one could be bothered to go into the shop most days. Nobody really needed flowers on the spur of the moment, and flower arrangements were ordered in advance.

She picked up the keys and went to the shop.

She unlocked the shop door, and started work.

Graham lay on his bed and thought about phoning Miranda. He was starting to feel a little depressed.

He had a theory about depression. He stared at the ceiling. Thinking up theories about depression stopped him feeling so depressed.

His house backed on to a field. Ever since Graham had remembered, he had seen, on the horizon, strolling couples, dog walkers, meandering teenagers and joggers. The joggers particularly interested him .What had interested him was where the fat had gone. He thought that when fat people got depressed, and they got depressed by being fat, they started to jog.

He had seen joggers passing by, from his window, and those who had lost their weight become chubby smiley creatures, then eventually the sort of man or woman who hung around beaches discussing the attributes of the sea surf, while admiring their own shapely surfboard type stomach. He saw this, but other people would wonder where the fat person had gone.

He thought their fat was layers of depression with minds of their own, like leeches. When the fatties went jogging, they lost the Depression Leeches in the gutter. The depression would then lay in wait, to attach itself to the nearest worried person, who in turn would get a little more depressed, who might eat more, (called 'feeding the depression'), until they got so fat and depressed they would start jogging. The cycle would begin again.

He reflected on his own present mood.

He must have been standing too near to the gutter.

He had a name for these little bits of depression; he called them, 'flobs.' Whenever he saw someone with their head low, shoulders hunched and sad looking, he would imagine that a flob had jumped out of the gutter on to the poor person's shoulder weighing him down. A flob slob. Once one flob was there, other flobs would be able to climb up and join their friends, and the person would get even more depressed and even fatter.

It made a lot more sense of his grandmother's sayings of 'standing tall will make you feel better,' and 'he's shaking off a depression.'

If he ever started to see the flobs, he would know he was hallucinating.

He went downstairs to watch the television. Do you phone someone, if they have stood you up?

Miranda sipped her tea, which was growing cold. It was growing cold outside too- there were splatters of rain drops on the café window. She had forgotten about 'Her Graham' and was staring at Mrs. Locks face. It had had lots of images over it, changing every few seconds. Her face was blurting at her. As if she wanted to tell her everything about herself. Miranda watched carefully.

She had an urge for Graham. He would laugh if he saw Mrs.Lock - a woman who listened to the computer tape, and had used it wisely. He would think she was the Coral Animate program.

Mrs. Lock shrugged at her. 'Have you never seen a woman eating before?' Her mouth tightened and a literal criss-cross pattern appeared around it looking like pre-school embroidery. Now she would have to be careful of Miranda, and she was just starting to like her. Women like her hid their 'woman eaten' with 'woman eating' or 'woman hating'.

The letter O appeared, in the same loose, linked, stitch way, just underneath her mouth. A needle shape started to grow by Mrs. Locks chin.

Miranda tried to hide a smile. 'Oh. Sorry. I was wondering about the water hardness in this area, and if my skin will look like yours when I get old. Your skin is very good quality.'

Mrs Lock looked at Miranda, with slit eyes. 'Are you gay, dear?'

Miranda reddened. 'No I am bloody well not. I was just looking at your bloody skin. There is not a lot else in here to look at, is there? Shall I stare at the counter? Hmm? Perhaps the draining board?'

'Is there any biscuits on the counter or the draining board? They might give you a bit of an appetite. You don't get fed a lot, do you, where you live?'

Mrs Lock still wanted to help the poor girl. It was only fair. She had bought her a cup of tea.

'Would *you* like some biscuits?' Miranda asked, with a bit of sarcasm.

A car appeared on Mrs. Lock's forehead, next to a stray grey curl. A Sarcasm detector. Miranda giggled.

Mrs Lock looked at her warily, and called the cook over. 'I'll have some biscuits. Have you got any butter shortbreads? No? They might be too rich for my stomach, have you got any digestives? Yes? Some of them, then.'

Miranda listened as Mrs. Lock's voice raised the tone of her voice. She sounded like a drag queen.

Mrs. Lock was trying to sound gay. She wanted to fit in. She didn't want Miranda to be lonely in years to come, just because she herself wasn't gay. She knew she would probably be switched within a week. There was always Switches spying. By next week the place would be swarming with gays, if she acted gay. If she behaved normally, it would be filled with old people. They wouldn't be much fun for a teenager like her.

'I haven't been able to eat biscuits since cook decided it was bad for our digestion. I used to love the ones with currents in, and the Peanut Delights always bought my taste buds alive.' She patted her rotund stomach. Best to pretend she lived in a OAP Home; that way she wouldn't get followed home by this strange woman. She had always thought Miranda was nice, but she was just... weird.

Miranda looked at Mrs. Lock carefully. Biscuit shapes appeared on her cheek. Miranda didn't care about what the cook's concern was over her bowel movements were, or what her favourite munch out of the biscuit tin was. She watched Mrs Locks face as she looked towards the kitchen, her eyes as innocent as a girls, bright with anticipation. The wrinkles around her eyes disappeared.

Mrs. Lock had the most extraordinary skin.

Mrs Lock looked back at Miranda. She really was odd. She would change the conversation and put her off her. Mrs Lock wasn't stupid Girls her age saw a pension book to steal, and house keys to nick. They hated claiming benefits, or going to work. Not that Mrs Lock was a pensioner, she just looked like one. 'So do you want to know anymore about 'her Graham'?'

Miranda leant back in her chair. She stared at her.

Mrs. Lock, unconcerned, was devouring her digestives, first by dipping them in her tea, then by sucking them.

Miranda felt tears spring into her eyes, and a feeling of angry sadness, which was quickly followed by disgust when she saw the mushy brown goo around Mrs. Lock's face. 'Oh, bloody hell. Can't you eat quieter?' Mrs. Lock blinked at her.

Mrs. Lock also felt a feeling, one of awkwardness, and she started to eat slower and louder, while Miranda watched angrily. When the last biscuit was eaten, her torso grew a little longer. She leant over, her head reaching Miranda's ear, where she burped, before resuming her accustomed shape.

'Do you know that your body became thinner, when you did that? ' Miranda was amazed, not scared. She was sitting with a real witch. An absolutely real witch. It was incredible.

Mrs. Lock stared at her with giant brown eyes, as large as owls. 'Haven't got a clue what you are saying.' Her eyes resumed normal dimensions, and become blue, as she continued, 'it's probably the light, or the clothes I am wearing. I'll ask cook. Mind you, she was wrong about the biscuits, so maybe I'll ask nurse instead.'

'Why does your face change shape.. So often? Your eyes? I thought it was the light too but … they change colour. You do know that, don't you?' Miranda said.

'Do they? Oh, I know what you mean. One of the nurses did mention to me that they look a little brighter in the right light. I'm not vain, but I'm sure if I had been a little younger, say, the same age as you. I would have had a chance with the men. Now, if you excuse me.'

She slurped at her tea, and picked up another biscuit. She was eager to go home. There was something Miranda was saying, something that she didn't want to remember.

She thought of her home, the white duvet room, the white living room, and her white laptop. She looked at Miranda accusingly. 'I had better go'

'That's a nice looking laptop, 'Miranda said slowly.

Mrs Lock looked at her. 'What?' Mrs. Lock didn't normally verbalise her thoughts.

'Mrs. Lock, think about Graham for me, could, you, but please don't talk with your mouth full'

She shoved a few more biscuits into Mrs. Lock's hand. 'Eat, and think.'

Mrs Lock looked at her carefully. If she could manoeuvre her hand around, she could call the police from her mobile. The woman was very weird.

But the other part of Mrs. Locks mind obeyed.

An image of Graham, and 'her Graham' appeared One was smaller than the other. One had a slightly squarer jaw. One had slightly larger lips. Seeing them together, Miranda could easily see the differences. It was embarrassing; how she mistook one for another.

Mrs. Lock was busy putting sugar packets in her pockets. She had an excuse to hide her mobile-phone-reaching. She looked up at her apologetically, when she felt Miranda looking. 'It'll save me from having to get up when I want sugar. Don't get cheeky with me about my over-nibbly appetite. Those slanty-eyed references to your biscuits are beginning to irritate me. '

'Really? 'Miranda said 'I didn't mean to be rude. Stay, and let me buy you lunch, and tell me about Graham, I meant to say. I am a bit nervous, that's all.

''Oh.' Mrs Lock answered, staring blankly out of the window.

Chapter 4

Arthur and Henry stared at the group of people at the end of the road.

'Arthur, do you still want to go no-fishing? Shall we do it today instead?'

Arthur nodded slowly.

The group were staring at the sky.

It was midmorning, and the sky was the same as every other year. One cloud was a mixture of numbers, '13 43 99', and one cloud was an arrow. The cloud angel had floated away, leaving them in its place. The group were taking photos and frowning at each other.

The village was never crowded. Something was wrong.

Henry looked at Arthur. 'Wait here for a mo, but open the car door.'

He walked over and prodded one on the arm.

The man he prodded looked at him, 'Do I know you?'

'Sorry. I thought.. Can I ask what..?'

But the man had already turned away.

Henry stared at the sky. The clouds were fluffy white, with a light blue background. There was nothing unusual about them. The cloud numbers and arrow were changing, as usual, in to a mouse.

He turned away, and walked back towards Arthur

'I don't think they have seen the sky before.'

Arthur looked at him. 'I don't think they are sky watchers. They are more like Switches planning mass murders. They are swarming.''

The group was silent. Henry and Arthur turned the corner, and walked quickly towards the lake. There was no car, but Henry thought it best to imply there was, in front of such a large group. The morning had been filled with too many people for him to feel comfortable with.

'Have we missed an important event, Henry? Perhaps in a forgotten calendar it is ''don't-point-at-the-sky'-but-take-severe-notice-of-it day.'…. Don't you dislike those people who stare at a person for a few seconds, then come back pretending they are him, years later? I think they are them. The man who showed them this place, and the man they watched, probably told them all to come back on the same day, years later, just so his own children could have a laugh at them, and take a photo. Watch out for old farmer Nothis, being a multitude, he would have said to his children, but at least it isn't my face back to haunt you.'

'Stop making excuses for the farmer Arthur. '

Arthur nodded.

It was probably true though. He could imagine an old conman taking money for arranging a child a future, then putting them all in a field, on the same day, and saying that is who the farmer was; themselves. That way they would blame themselves instead of him. Self-accusation was an old conman trick.

It was all mentioned in one of Arthur's old pamphlet, on 'how to be a Switch'; loose all the guilt by losing the victim in a hall of mirrors made by them selves.

It could be the old faux farmer who created a crowd, as if by magic.

But it could have been something else.

Arthur made a note to look at old maps of the area, to see what was there before the pub was built and what used to be at the end of the street. As, if self-farming wasn't that reason that they were all there, then they might think they were queuing in advance for a Half fpoon Of Johsons Lemming Ude. There had probably had

80

been an establishment of serious shopping, in front of them, that had been knocked down, leaving them to look at the sky on a return journey, rather than billowing curtains.

It would be back. Everything always comes back. Good ideas were never thrown away, but circulated until the original inventor couldn't claim it was theirs anymore.

They were just re-establishing pre-re-building knowledge of the area, perhaps.

Arthur sighed. He was scared of them, and always had been. He suffered from Ochlophobias. Ochlophobias was plural because he had a phobia of lots of crowds, not just one. There is nothing more frightening for him that a gang of Switches, a coven of cults, and a bunch of festival goers all deciding to walk in the same direction at the same time.

They would fight.

He started to twitch. The memory of the crowd in the pub was catching up on him. Like with most people with phobias he had the ill- effects after the event. If he had been scared of spiders, he would have been the type to put the spider outside, before jumping on a chair and screaming. He would have also showered compulsively for a few hours afterwards too, he supposed. And perhaps he would have had a shave. His face reminded him of the back of a skull spider when he was hairy, so he pitied those men with arachnophobia. I suppose they didn't make very good stalkers either, if their twins had beards. They would probably run off, hands waving and shouting 'Ahhrrr' , thinking the two day growth was spider-related.

He revised his opinion of stalking arachnophobes to include the image of them screaming and pointing at barber shop windows and at musical festival customers. Were aracnophobes also scared of spider webs, and associated images? Would one run off screaming if he wore a cling film scarf? (He thought that would sort of look like spider-webs - early morning dew type spider webs.)

What scares crowds off? They must have at least one accumulated fear. Perhaps it was being on their own.

He was shaking. He never knew what to do after he met a crowd, so his hands sort of fumbled around each other. Because he had met two crowds, in such a short time, his feet sort of fumbled around too. His skin, not as lively or interesting as Mrs Locks, but still artistic, drew spiders on his ankle, followed by lots of dots. The dots represented bits on socks.

Arthur would start scratching his ankle soon.

Miranda was thinking, while Mrs. Lock, full on biscuits and tea, looked curiously around her. She never looked at cafes much, but it was always wise to check the skirting boards to make sure the place was clean. Tomato sauce stains on the walls were a good indication that there were ant droppings in the sugar bowl too.

She wasn't normally one of life's gawpers. She looked out of the window, to see if the glass was clean too. Messages written on dirty windows were always a sign of unhygienic cooks. Well, not a sign, but a definite indication. When the finger writing spelt 'help' it was best not to go in at all.

She was starting to get wind.

Miranda, with a look of distaste, stared at her stomach, then up at her face. She reluctantly smiled at the image of a window imprinted on Mrs. Locks face. 'And after we have had a salad, I think a plate of pasta, and perhaps a side dish. Mrs. Lock, are you listening to me?'

Mrs. Lock nodded. She wasn't that interested. She was wondering where the café owner bought his paint. . 'What colour would you call that? 'She answered. She pointed at the edging around the café walls. The owner probably bought it off the internet.

Miranda tried to control her temper. 'Rose pink. Well? Are you listening?'

Mrs. Lock tutted. She pretended to fuss over the tea cups. 'Of course I am. I'm just trying to think of the right thing to say.'

Miranda took a deep breath. 'I only asked what you would like for lunch, not telling you about a recent demise.'

Mrs. Lock thought for a moment. Why was it that all the people she ever met only talked about food? She was always beleaguered by people and their dietary habits. It was either what, or who, they were about to eat, what she should eat, or what others were eating.

Why couldn't people suggest seeing a work of art or going to a museum, rather than talking about food?

She never used to talk about food, but she had started to talk about it, and eat copious amounts of it after years in their company.

She didn't care about her weight and mostly avoided the mirror herself. Vanity gave rise to Narcissism, she thought. Keeping herself away from the mirror meant she kept away from her twin too. She wouldn't be letting hers in, in the middle of night.

It isn't because she thought that mirror-staring was wrong. All the best advice recommended avoidance for just young people, who were still growing, and for people looking for a sexual partner. 'Both were susceptible to self-love more than the average person' was the general advice.

She always used the pocket mirror. If she did start to love her own reflection then her twin would have to have a head the size of a tennis ball. She only saw one eye at a time, so she supposed that her twin would have to have only one giant eye too.

Mrs. Lock inwardly reddened. She had all those thoughts about the mirror, when all she really wanted to remember was what the girl's name was.

'Yes. That sounds fine Miranda.' She narrowed her eyes at the girl.

Perhaps it was because Miranda was trying to be her mirror, with her over observant glances. Something on her cheek! 'Mirror-and-her' is what her name was!

She was probably sent by a twin Switch, to persuade her to be a proper, fully fledged Switch.

Mrs. Lock would have to think about this. She thought she was the person who was doing the persuading, not the woman opposite. It had been a trap.

She had hidden herself for so long, she had forgotten what envy, hatred, and jealousy her face received. It wasn't because she was beautiful; it was because one face follows another. When she didn't succumb to the tribal cult, all the faces similar to hers failed to see the charm of cult-living too. It was the way they had been taught; to mimic the person they wanted to replace, so they couldn't help not wanting to replace her because she wouldn't.

For a while there had been a rebellion against the Switches and she had hidden. They had all hidden. They hid by showing no opinion. They hid behind a polite veneer disguised by a thin smile, but they didn't physically hide by running or moving. It is difficult to run from the enemy when the enemy could be everyone. Besides running from everyone would mean a fortune spent in trainers, sport socks and foot deodorant. She just couldn't afford it.

Miranda leaned a little closer. She couldn't be sure but she thought she saw a blouse collar on Mrs. Locks cheek, as if she wanted to pull her top up to hide her head. There were several collars on her cheek.

Mrs. Lock associated colour with 'killer'. She never wore tones of red with blue and green. That was like agreeing with the worse.

Mrs. Lock chewed slowly on some grated carrot. The woman

opposite was still staring at her, when she thought Mrs. Lock wasn't looking.

Switches seemed to single her out for negative attention, since back then, but they were like that with everyone. They snapped and snarled in a characteristic manner. It was only when they began to say her name, without being told it, that she guessed they were still stalking.

She looked back down at the mixed leaf salad. Miranda was busy eating. There was no movement in her face as she chewed.

Mrs. Lock could tell Miranda was affected by her own name by the way she was not moving her mouth.

Her mirror was always with her, and she had changed it to her own self-portrait.

Arthur would have said Miranda was a victim of the namists too. When she lied to herself, which was often, Henry would presume that the Switches had been leaning against walls, or lying on the grass, as she passed. Arthur would check outside with the CCTV, and usually he was right. Her name would have been acted out, 'a mirror, laying on it's back,' or 'leaning'. That's lying to herself. She had been a victim of misconstrued uses of her name. The youths only appeared if Miranda followed the same routine. He knew it wasn't coincidental.

Eileen had overslept, after she had already risen from her bed and after she had already eaten her breakfast.

She slept quite easily by never over-eating. Breakfast had been an apple. Her energy levels were always low, meaning that if she ever became worried or distressed, she would instantly fall asleep, no matter where she was. She cat napped when there was a thunderstorm, when cakes refused to rise, and when a bill was due.

She woke quite easily too, because her mind was alert for intruders. Unfortunately, as soon as her eyes opened at a noise, they would instantly shut again because of all the worry and distress an intruder would cause. She slept heavier if a neighbour banged a door shut.

She fell back to sleep instantly.

When she woke up again, she thought about cleaning, but, with an angry look about, she decided not to. Miranda would appear and complain about the smell. She complained about everything. She complained about Eileen dusting, even. She liked the spiders, and their webs. She liked dead moths and unexplained smudges on the white walls. Sometimes, Eileen had thought, she was more a fictional witch than a witch was, despite always protesting the opposite. Henry made up excuses for her messiness. He said it was because they were Very English. They had British flags in cupboards, and Jubilee Mugs. She had been subliminally altered by the map they lived on being shaped like a pig. She wanted to live in a pig pen. It is to do with her conviction she is human, and British, he said.

Eileen could see that. She could see how knowing you are human could turn you into a pig. Not.

Miranda didn't think piggy thoughts. She just liked watching the spiders. They talked to her, she thought, using body movements. She also liked to think the smudges on the walls were messages from their miniature world. All she wanted was for Eileen to wait for them to finish spelling out what they wanted to say, before dusting them down.

From 'The Book Of Words.'
Up-and-down bouncy spiders; A strange arachnid that does

press ups, dances, and swings the upper half of it's body around from one leg, while hanging from a ceiling. It gives the appearance of a ball being swung round on the end of a piece of string, before it 'springs' forward to attack. It doesn't seem to know how big it is, as it tries to head butt it's prey. Some think, though, that they do know what their size ratio is compared to a human, and are attempting to explain to the humans, and animals, by mimicry, that spiders themselves cause no damage to the mammal form, and are in fact helping the larger animals by eating fleas, so why the hell do mammals keep head-butting them for? It might not hurt them, but it bloody hurts spiders, when it's the other way round. Some people accuse the Up-and-down bouncy spiders as being overly sarcastic, when they are acting out their hurts.

The spiders are mistakenly thought to be the close companion of the switches because of their similarity in the way they communicate, but the Switches disliked them intensely because of their similar behaviour.

(Also, they, the Switches, are expert mimers, and they think they understand the jumpy-up-and-down spiders too well. What they think the spiders are charade-ing out is mostly quite disgustingly rude and nasty.)

The spiders are also called the 'Helter-Skelter' spider in America. They become most famous for their part in forming a 'cult'. (After seeing the spiders move about the following comments were noted, 'I'm either hallucinating it or that man just made that spider dance, walk on two legs, then bounce up and down...' 'ahhr.. It's just done an impersonation of a juggler. ')

Normally the jumpy-up-and-downs appeared after or before tropical weather and mosquitoes, so were also seen as OMENS.

COLOUR; white, then striped brown.   As if, said some

biologists very quietly, so not to cause hysteria, they were larger, wingless mosquitoes. As well as their colour change there was also mysterious zoom-zoom marks found on nearby people, and things, that gave substance to this theory. Some of the jumpy-up-and-downs hide their extra long legs underneath them. You know the sort of spider -bites you in one place while tapping you on the shoulder in another place – similar to the 'crone's claw spider' aka 'electrical spider', which has one extra long leg, shaped like an index finger, especially grown for shoulder tapping. It gives tiny electrical shocks to other insects. Normally lives in the air vent.

Eileen thought the spiders were getting bigger every year. She could tell by the marks on the table; there were several semi-circle scratches, the size of dinner plates, etched into the wood. Even though they were probably were made by dinner plates she picked up the insect killer and sprayed underneath the table top.

Then she rested her head back on the table top and slept again.

Miranda looked at Mrs. Lock's forehead. 'U R A '. Miranda waited, trying not to look impressed or surprised. The letters disappeared, and a light switch appeared, with a question mark next to it.
 Miranda reddened. She wasn't a Switch. She didn't curse. She knew she wasn't one. No one had tried to sell her a fake identity. No one had commented on her similarity to another person, or called her by a different name to the one she had. She would never be a Switch. Or a witch. Real witches didn't exist, except for the old woman sitting opposite her. She might be one. They were fallacies. Or phallic. She could never remember the correct word.

88

'BOOK OF WORDS;

Witches, and Switches, or Switches that are also Witches aren't magical or telepathic. They are a chain reaction. If one looks angry, then the angry face is repeated until it tails out. This is a 'curse'.

It is, they presume, the victims fault if they are a victim of a curse, because they should know not to stand where a memorised curse happens.

When someone curses, (the word 'curse' can be written into it's long hand form; 'C' is 'see', 'urs' is 'us' and 'e' is ' me' . = 'see us/me'), it is normally in the form of a repeated gesture or look from a repeated face. It is presumed that if a person has done something bad to the 'faces' that they will eventually apologise, rather than see the same curse from the same persons for years to come.

Switches, and Witches, who have no charm or persuasion about them, and copy what they see with no thought pattern to interrupt their mimicry, are used to spread the curse too. They do not curse other Switches, because they do not want to offend another group of Switches, as they do not know how many people are in that other group. Cursing another Switch might start a war. They did individuals, or people who stood in the wrong place. People who stood in the wrong place must be new, they thought, to stand in the wrong place, so they couldn't be a Switch that was expected anywhere.

Switches, and Witches, were generally cowards.

☼

The next entry was.

Book of Words:
'Cats keep themselves clean, but never clean their claws, so why are their claws so clean?'

☼

.

Mrs. Lock looked at Miranda wearily. She would really have to get out of this change-a-letter-lifestyle. Always Switches and witches.

Miranda seemed to be both.

She would Switch her, then if no one noticed, then Witch her, probably. That was; she would swap and then eat her.

Miranda was still studying her with an intimacy that was inappropriate but, admitted Ms. Lock, there was an element of individuality in the stares that normally wasn't associated with the Switches.

Miranda wasn't trying to convey anything to her.

She wasn't trying to catch her eye, in that gay kind of way either. but seemed to be having some kind of communication with bits of her face.

Mrs. Lock never thought that her cheek may have an individual lifestyle, without her.

She thought back to what she knew of witches.

They talked normally. They didn't mess about with 'guess-my-motive-and-objective' kind of no-speak. They didn't play 'guess-my-vowel' or 'what-is-her-name'. Their behaviour seemed quite normal too, but then, compared to the Switches, everyone else seemed normal. For a possible victim she supposed witches looked like saviours, and the voice of reason. That is, if the choice was only between the two.

But she only got her knowledge from children's story books. They wore pointy hats too, like Switches, but not with the same brim. Theirs were black, but not because they were auditioning to be cult leader, and they had warts on big noses. They had a lot

90

of toads too. They put humans in big black pots to cook, and read old books of spells, at midnight.

Mrs. Lock scratched her head. Now she thought of it, those books may have been a bit of baby propaganda. The TV was no more informative. Only Miranda's mum looked as if she gained her information from the same place.

Mrs. Lock herself had been raised as... Mrs Lock blinked. She could not remember.

She reached for her plate of pasta. It was because she was so skinny that her memory was bad.

Malnutrition did that to some people. She looked over to where her closed pocket mirror sat. Her cheekbones had looked almost the same as Miranda's. She looked at her with pity.

'Have some more crispy & crumbly breaded mushrooms' she urged, waving a side dish in front of her.

Witches in general avoided the sun because their skin would take a photograph of what was around them. If they tried to show they had been in the sunlight, their skin would become too warm. Not like usual skin, that reddens, but with images of the sun itself, that would blister to show the shape and heat of the sun. People with sun burn were not witches. They were people with sun burn. Witches, like vampires, would grow old and wrinkle instantly, and have sun icons to tell the world that the sun had done it.

Mrs. Lock kept her head down, most of the time. She had been a sunny baby, too scared of losing her identical parents in their world of identical people, to disobey them, and they had said that she mustn't sit in the sun, else she would burn. So she didn't. She used fifty protection sun block and kept her face away from it. She kept herself covered, and walked in the shade.

Her face, unknown to her, still showed what her eyes had seen, or what she imagined beyond her line of vision.

Her cheeks elongated, to resemble the neck she had just looked at, and neck bands appeared on her forehead. She was old, and starving, when she looked in the mirror, after walking with her head down.

It was raining. Mrs. Lock looked again. That was what was nudging her thoughts. It never rained on Mouse Morning. Not in this part of the country.

She remembered that much, as she sucked spaghetti strands.

She didn't trust any of the story book people. Those witches that Miranda lived with made the horizon their broomsticks. Well, not them, because they lived here, but their look-a-likes did. They would disappear over the hill, down one of the 'A' roads after a day of pretend shopping. Either that, or they would loiter about, looking for a familiar face, to say, 'You're-our-son,' to. That was the words most similar to 'horizon' and they liked to rhyme. Strangely, it was mostly women wearing low cut tops, and very short skirts that said this. Mrs Lock thought they were trying to sell themselves. They would have had more luck calling the men 'good looking', or 'handsome', rather than a child born to them, she thought, but perhaps they were auditioning for the position of mother witch.

She avoided them when she could.

They thought, bizarrely, that she was competition, or, and she shivered slightly at the idea, they thought she was food.

Mostly they were homeless, persuaded to travel away from their legal homes to see their faces outlined in the skies above. Most of the witch switch faces were in the air, in cloud formation, year after year.

They forgot their own birthdays and instead celebrated when the image of their own face appeared above them.

She didn't know where they got their food. She mostly saw them from her window, or saw the back of their shoes as she walked.

Having her head constantly down had its advantages.

She knew them from the colour of their socks, and the flare of their trousers. They knew her by the colour of her hat top. They didn't know her features.

She had kept away from them, but had watched as they settled where their false cloud-idol appeared the longest.

Mrs. Lock looked over her plate.

Miranda didn't resemble anyone of the sky people, as she called those Switch witches. She didn't have a Nose, nose. It was an average nose. Un-spectacular, and not a nose to point at. Noses used to be a big thing. Mrs Lock was old enough to remember that a wagging finger meant 'no' *just* because the finger followed the *length* of the nose. A shaking head also meant 'no' because the eyes followed the *breadth* of the nose.

Miranda's nose was small.

Mrs. Lock's nose was small too.

She looked normal. Well, like a normal Switch. She blended in. She was low-level maintenance. Nothing about her was interesting. She didn't sparkle with slightly oiled hair, and it didn't bounce with natural energy. Her clothes were a sort of washed out, non-noticeable colour, bought from charity shops.

She was the background to everyone's stardom. She always had been since… Mrs. Lock looked out of the café window.

Since…

She couldn't remember. The rain was glittering in the sun, and there were people outside. Lots of people.

Rain, sun, and lots of people were unusual, in the Moment of the Spoon.

The Moment of the Spoon evolved from the Mouse Cloud. The cloudy tail swung gently round to meet the cloud stomach of the cloud mouse, and the cloudy body of it disappeared, leaving a line, that made the spoon's handle. It was the Moment of the Spoon.

No wonder there were lots of people outside, in the rain, and not in the café itself.

She guessed they didn't want a literal interpretation of the combined clouds. Some people may take the cloud's five second appearance as a command to do something with the two separate cloud images, as if it was the moment of a conception and they had to combine the two pictures into one image, to last forever, or at least four a long time.

If those people were cooks in a kitchen, it may mean a mouse in the soup. It had happened before.

Mrs. Lock pushed the bowl away and looked back at the window.

All the people outside were wearing grey. This was very odd.

She looked back at Miranda, and nodded her head in the direction of the window. 'Can you see them?'

Witches were revered by some of the Switches because they looked different. The Switches wanted to be more like them; individual.

There was more chance of them surviving than there was for a Switch because instead of a thousand witches born every minute, there was probably one witch born every minute.

There was always something different about a witch. It was normally the nose. Noses were safe when it came to gentle unknown evolutionary steps of the genes. They weren't a continuation like other parts of the body. They had a definite full stop, in case anything went wrong. Genes could relax, knowing there was a nostril in the way.

Switches that admired witches were mostly plain themselves but wanted their unborn children to have that special nostril look, so they wouldn't have to worry about their safety as much. They stared at witches' noses with a myopic concentration in much the same way that Miranda was staring at Mrs. Lock, hoping that their own genetic inheritance would surprise them with a bit of individuality.

If their own genetics decided to have a quick change of direction, then they hoped it would be in the nose area, anyway. The nose was a harmless detour that would hopefully leave the body complete and able.

Other witches hoped the same – the witches that were born less-able, – and they stared at noses with the same concentration as a Switch would, hoping all their unspent angles and rounds would go to the nasal area and stay there.

Nose-staring was quite trendy for a while, and so were beauty spots and knobbly knees. Knobbly knees were particular popular because they could be hidden. The fashion for rolling up one trouser leg so the knobbly knee could be observed by the mother-to-be was a casual pastime for people with particularly outstanding knobbles.

Most Switches thought that they were who they saw, which was understandable. They were identical to thousands of others, who looked exactly the same but who were not relations. This is why some of them hoped that by staring at others it would change their child's features, just a little bit. Most of the Switches that felt this way were a bit secretive of their yearnings because... well, they were Switches. Switches were well known for their identical looks and lifestyles.

It was as if they were rebelling by showing maternal concern for their unborn child's safety and were raising doubts that other Switches could be trusted, by their yearning for a bit of individuality.

Rebelling was considered nasty and vindictive by the Switch cult, and practitioners of staring were watched closely for signs of opposition.

The starers had to start buying clandestine photos of knee poses and thoughtful hawk-type nasal displays and hide them under their universal-use cloaks, so they weren't caught by Switch purists.

Switch purists believed that if there were no witches in the world, there would be no illness or disease. They believed, whole heartedly, that they *were what they saw*, so refused to have what they called a 'deformity' in front of their faces; they refused to be in the presence of witches. The sight of them might contaminate their purity, they said.

The purists abhorred difference and embraced cult thinking with narrow minded self adoration. Self was all, and all was self, was their motto. They thought they were natural, like groups of birds, or cows, or lions, with their identical looks. Witches were aberrations.

They warned less compliant Switches that one more step in the nose-envy direction and they would be back in the half-beast world, eating with hooves, or trying to fly with shoulder blades and no legs. That is what hoping to be different gave you, they preached, nothing but turn-back limbs, and no eyebrows.

They weren't limiting self-damaged genes by nasal envy, but encouraging it, the purists said, with their want to be different.

Mrs. Lock was undecided about their lecturing. Their whole lives had been about themselves, and their mirrors. They weren't genetic scientists, or biologists. They were too extreme in voicing their opinion to be believable. They had probably spotted a witch that owned a better make of mobile phone than them, so were being persecuting.

If they couldn't swap places with someone, they would destroy them, and scavenge through their possessions, so she wasn't surprised at their anti-witch statements. Wealth was their real target. They were the same hatred towards the qualified, the talented, and the skilled.

Once they had been destroyed, they could step in their shoes.

She thought of the backs of shoes she had seen. She had never had shoe envy, like some people. She wasn't a shoe fetisher. She had been born when shoes were relatively cheap. That sort of meant, colloquially, that every one was good at something, so enjoyed each others skills, and no one was envious about imagined riches. The reason they weren't envious was because everyone could quite easily calculate expenses and the cost of living: a rich person was probably left with the same amount of money a poor person had, relatively speaking. If a poor person wanted to go for an occasional swim, it would cost less than four pound. If a wealthy person wanted to go for an occasional swim, it would cost them half a million for the house, gardens and pool, an unknown security risk by inviting a pool cleaner in, and the price of a private life guard, should they want the full benefits of relaxation.

 Some people still tried to squash their unsuitable feet into others shoes, though, with an insane yearning to believe they could be someone else, through ID theft. Mrs. Lock thought their main problem and why they wanted wealth was because they wanted servants. She could tell. They were so dominating. It was a Switch thing, to do with their baby persona. She guessed that they thought that people would *know* they *weren't babies* if they didn't have servants, otherwise they would be able to fool them. For people who looked in the mirror constantly, they were really stupid.

Anyway, to be safe, when it come to witches noses, Mrs Lock balanced envy with sensible avoidance. Other people's knowledge may have been gleaned through rifled scientist's papers, rather than listening to soap operas.

Mrs. Lock didn't recognise that she was unusual herself.

She was an open secret in the Switches community, one that was used to identify friends from strangers, but she had a mental block when it came to herself.

97

When she was born she had been treated with care and deference. Her parents had looked at her curiously, as had everyone. The curious looks did not stop, and Mrs. Lock became to regard them as usual. She was usually over protected from the sun, when she was inside and outside of the house, but that was all. She was always nourished, but when she looked in the mirror she always looked under-fed, and thought that was the cause of concern.

Mrs Lock thought she had bare skin too; skin that was naked of words and thought. There was not a blemish in sight when she looked at a mirror. It was skin that didn't talk back. It wouldn't pull a face at an audience if she didn't like your perfume.

She had seen skin-talkers herself, on London tubes and in bus queues. Their skin didn't have physical lips or anything like that, but showed pictures, letters and numbers to convey thoughts that should be, in her opinion, kept in their minds. She was wary of them, as much as she was of witches. They looked too much like movie vampires to be comfortable with, with whitened faces due to too much sun tan lotion, and they talked behind their friends backs on their own backs where everyone could see. Vampires were the same. Vampires didn't drink blood. They had *thinking* blood that talked for them too.

They were as unpopular with some Switches as witches were, because copying them was too difficult as well. Skin that talked was harder to impersonate than a witches' characteristics. A fake plastic nose was straightforward. A fake beauty spot was also trouble-free. Painting on shaped rouge and washing it off to replace it a few seconds later, in an endless circle, was a bit tiring and less convincing.

Her own body had been checked as a baby, to make sure she was

98

easily swappable, and again at puberty by the 'Community Hall Ritual Meeting For the Cleansing the Community.' where everyone had to strip off and check each other for lively warts.

Her skin hadn't even grimaced at the sight of so many nosy people. In self preservation, it had hid away from the stares of others, fully aware she would be ostracised from the community of Switches if it was known she was more like a train dweller than she was like them.

But when she was with her family, or feeling safe, it developed like an old sepia photo, or as if she had used a flesh coloured pen over herself, a shade darker than her skin tone. On her forehead she showed them a forecast of the imaged-clouds that would appear that day. She would show lions, men, women, houses, mice, eyes, spoons, numbers, and letters, depending on what the predicted clouds looked like. Her forehead showed them the sky, for the whole year, every year.

It wasn't just her forehead that portrayed images, but all of her skin. It showed thoughts and ideas, portraits and maths problems.

Her parents, pleased when she was born, thought that Mrs. Lock shouldn't look at herself too much, because she reflected what she saw, so her reflection would reflect back the same image which would develop on top of the same image. Her images might develop into three dimensional ones. Three dimensional lumps wasn't a pleasing thought.

.

.

Chapter 5

'What does the woman look like?' Eileen interrupted. 'Is she about five foot nine inches, thin lips, thin face, and incredibly overweight?'

The café owner nodded 'Yes.' He said. 'I suppose she is. It isn't that as much as..'

'Yes' said Eileen interrupting. 'I know. Thanks for telling me. I will have a couple of apple pies off you next week, and a reservation for two on the ninth.'
Eileen put the phone down.
She went red.
She studied her tea-cup.
Eileen remembered Mrs. Lock.
Mrs. Lock had appeared once or twice at their community hall gatherings.
Not in this town, but her home town.
The community hall gatherings were a strip off and bare all get together. It was supposed to be an identity check, but in reality it was just an excuse to see who was the most gullible. It was only after her first flush of youth she realised that. It did mean, though, that she hadn't made a fool of herself chatting up the fat boy who lived at the farm, who turned out to be a woman with an incontinence pad. And it did make her feel less nervous of the local policeman, who had a scar on his buttock.
She didn't know how it became a devil worshipping group. She guessed one thing led to another. One moment there is a crotchet and knitting circle, the next moment, after a second or two of

exaggerations, they have a javelin pole in their hand with a knight in full wired armour on the end of it.

She guessed it started to be called a Deaf-all group, when they all stopped talking, and started to use their eyes instead. It was supposed to add a bit of mystery to a dull evening, even if it was contrary to the point of the get-together. Voicing an accent would sort of help identify each other, wouldn't it?

Anyway, Eileen had been a regular attendee, and Mrs. Lock had been the highlight of the devil worshipping gossip, but only when she wasn't at the devil worshipping group.

Her skin was alive, in a way the community had never seen before. It chatted away with no discrimination, when Mrs. Lock wasn't thinking. She had stunned them all with it, and had continued to stun them. She was full of pictograms and an awful lot of food.

It hadn't been Eileen, but one of the girls, who said she was Mrs. Lock's cousin, who had insisted that Mrs Lock be exposed for the train dweller she should be. She had obviously been swapped without the approval of the whole group, she said. And the other members of the community spied on Mrs. Lock, to confirm her tube-station status. They stalked her, mercilessly, until she finally snapped at them.

Then they had to lie, and say they were recruiting for their secret group.

'Well, it isn't a secret then, is it?' she had said, and had told her parents. Her parents, aware of local rituals, had then told her about the Switch meetings.

Her skin, strangely, had suggested, in clear Ariel font, that she attended, and her parents, still amazed at Mrs. Locks talking skin, reluctantly agreed.

Mrs. Lock herself didn't understand why her parents decided to send her to a devil worshipping group. She had no idea what her subconscious said most of the time.

She understood about identity checking but standing around in a community hall, naked, didn't seem to have much to do with her identity. They were all mostly identical to each other, with only their clothes to differate them, so why would she want to take them off? And there was no way she was coupling near the cutlery draw, if they were using the identity parade as an excuse for a quick sexual encounter.

Mrs. Lock had thought she would have to stop attending the village fete if that is what they did. She didn't like the idea of pubic hair on the blue willow pattern.

Anyway it had obviously started as a meeting group for skin talkers, she thought, and she didn't really feel comfortable about going. They really could be identified by stripping off. She just felt embarrassed by their blatant lack of ritual knowledge.

When she had finally got to the community hall gathering, everyone attending – and it had been the biggest gathering the group had seen – had been one of the people who had stalked her.

Mrs. Lock hadn't really noticed. She was busy deciding that it was like infant school changing rooms, but with a lot more hair. She'd be fine as long as none of them showed her a finger painting of the sun. Painted with a flourish of lemon-yellow powder paint.

Eileen herself had manoeuvred herself close enough, during a shopping outing, to see a cup and saucer appear on Mrs. Lock's cheek. Mrs. Lock's skin had become less shy, over the years.

It had gently persuaded the local community it was normal by showing itself in short periods of brief exposure, followed by longer bouts of exhibitionism. Most people didn't think twice about seeing her skin, and as she seemingly had no idea of it herself, as they were just as easily persuaded that she was still a

Switch, even if her skin wasn't.

Some purer Switches, locally and from other counties, had been invited to witness Mrs. Lock's revelation. About half thought they were too Pure to look, and had worn balaclavas the wrong way round, so they didn't expose themselves to the influence of a skin-changer, which was worse, in their opinion, than a witch with big ears or big noses, or a vampire with pointy teeth.

The group had their scenario all planned out, but then...
Mrs. Lock had appeared.
And her skin was.... nothing. It was the same as theirs. Not even a mole to indicate a witch or vampire nature.

Eileen reddened again, a deeper shade of redness.
They had then all accused Mrs. Lock of not being herself, but a double, which of course confused everyone. The gatherings were for Switches, so why penalise someone for being a Switch? They said it silently, and everyone caught the gist, except for Mrs. Lock, who was busy looking at the community hall kitchen, hoping for an open window, in case she needed an easy escape.

The other Switch communities stopped talking to the village, thinking they were Switch- finders sent by the unemployment office.

Eileen tutted and closed the curtains. It was raining. Raining was messy, especially on spoon day. She didn't want to see it. Or those people staring up at the sky. They were messy too. They were in the wrong place setting. They should be in town, not standing outside her house, looking up at the sky. They were getting wet.
She fell asleep, just as she was wondering why they were there.

Graham was sitting on his bed. He was missing Miranda.

He would have to phone her, and see why she didn't turn up. It was just that it was so peaceful without her being next to him. She was all danger, instead of all angel.

He stood up, undecided. His phone was on the bookshelf, with a dead battery. If he plugged it in, he could phone her.

He reached for it and there they were, in the peripheral of his vision; about two hundred people. They were in the lane where the flobby joggers normally stood.

All looking at the sky.

Perhaps they had possession of a photo of loads of footprints, left by the joggers, taken years ago, but hadn't realised it was the footprints of joggers.

Perhaps they had mistaken the photo as hundreds of people who stood in fields, so hundreds of people had decided that is where they belonged.

They might be waiting to see what their photo-feet-twin predecessors had done next.

The looking up movement could mean they had heard of flobs too. They were standing tall, so no flobs could climb up them.

Graham sighed. He was becoming self-obsessed. They didn't know how he thought.

He looked outside again, and wondered if he should take a photo. He decided not to, in case the same type of social historians found it. They would probably decide that the grouping were looking at a band, not the sky, and before Graham would know what was happening, there would be a festival going on behind his back garden, and socks thrown over the fence.

Socks over the fence were a bad sign. It meant trespassers had already claimed to have jumped the barrier, and had been left un-reprimanded.

Graham moved closer to the window, to see if any sock activity had already happened.

There were no socks. He turned his head to look at what they were staring at. They were looking at the cloud spoon. But there was something just beyond it. Another cloud, that seemed to be raining by itself. The sun, and a rainbow behind it, made the rain multi-coloured, like fractioning jewels.
The people were all standing tall and still, like rows of carved rock, staring.
.
He would phone Miranda tomorrow instead. He quickly looked through the clothes in his wardrobe, and grabbed a grey coat.
He ran down the stairs.

Miranda had seen the same as Graham, but from the window of the café. She had seen a grey crowd, anyway.
It wasn't the same grey crowd but if you weren't that thoughtful about the village, you could mistake one hill top for another hill top, so could mistake all the grey crowds as just being the one grey crowd.

If you were a witch you had to know things like that. The ability to stand on one hill top, but be seen from several different

106

directions was very useful if you are alone in a world full of Switches. It made it look as if there were lots of witches, not just one. Prophets and Saints did the same thing, before the television was invented.

The sight of one, apparently seen all over the place, at the same time started the rumour of an omnipotent presence. A hill in the centre of three unconnected villages, and telescopes helped.

If you were a Switch, the opposite was true. A village surrounded by identical roads or hills was the perfect place to look as if there were less rather than more.

Miranda had looked at her mobile phone with a disinterested glance, but hadn't thought to pick it up and photograph the multitude. The strange long term effect of TV on her had been that when something camera-needy happened, she didn't use a camera. People didn't use mobile phone cameras on the television; it spoilt the plot line.

If the cook had suddenly announced 'Face book' Miranda would have instantly realised the situation needed a camera.

It was social conditioning that did that. Miranda didn't even use Facebook, but the tentacles of internet browsing had snagged her. When Mrs. Lock had drawn her attention to the people outside she had noticed that a high percentage were male, that was all. She didn't think they were out of place, just that one had a particularly nice shade of blonde coloured hair.

And another had a nice build.

Mrs. Lock nervously played with the sugar packets again, putting a few sachets in her pocket.

The situation was reminiscent of something in the past. The grey clothing was what staid her eyes on the group, and that was what was bringing back memories.

Their clothes were ironed. That meant they weren't car dwellers, If they had one contact in the village, there was no way that one contact could have ironed hundreds of pieces of grey clothing for

107

this display of stand-in-the-rain sky starers. She was ill at ease.

Mrs.Lock suddenly stood up.
She opened the café door
And she started walking.
A slow smile spread through the group outside, as they made a
space for her.

Henry and Arthur reached the lake just as the first drops of
vibrant rain fell.
They were hiding.
Something new had happened, and it wasn't nice. Nothing new
ever happened and even though it was very dull and dangerous, it
meant dangerous events could be predicted and avoided because
they were old events.

If a car always skidded on the thirteenth, at five am, everyone
driving a car would avoid the area, and time, where the vehicle
normally skidded.

New events caused chain reactions. If someone new bought an
extra portion of chips at the chip shop, a bag of potatoes would
have to be opened to accommodate the whim. The local chip
consumption was carefully calculated so that sacks of potatoes
were not left open overnight. Open bags of food led to rat
invasions, and then to food poisonings, the villagers felt. They
lived too near the fields to take a risk.

The children were frowned on if they swung on the swings
longer than their allotted ten minutes each. The swing fixer
visited only once a year, and do you know how annoying that
squeak is, once it starts? They were told.

And so on.

Henry and Arthur had heard it since they were children themselves. Whims should be acted on when they were in the town, not in the village. Whims were new things.

The crowds were new, the rain was new, and being slightly stalked was new for them too.

Arthur was wondering if it was a chain reaction of newness. Should he expect another 'new'? He looked around nervously.

Henry nodded to the path they had just left. 'Do you think she is still following?'
Arthur shook his head. 'No, but it would be better to text Eileen and tell her we had a Miranda foot-stepping us. She will probably try her next.'
Henry nodded. He had forgotten that some of the Switches were so literal. The look-a like had stepped out of the pub, just as they reached the corner. She had looked around, and once she had spotted them, had started to follow. The foot gate had confused her though. They never used it, but went to the path that dipped down.
Once they were hidden by the trees, she had turned back, puzzled.
It hadn't been an invite, Henry had wanted to say, but he didn't want to encourage her further. For people who weighed and judged every word before it was spoken, no word was ever said in an impromptu and meaningless way. Their attitude to words was the same as some others had to personal possessions, but as they had no personal possessions, words become their possessions instead.
Henry hadn't realised that people like her still existed. He must

have stressed his words too emphatically without realising. He hadn't cursed for a long time, and was out of practise.

She was the type to want paying. He could tell. She wasn't the usual Miranda look-a-like, if she followed him like that. Henry was beginning to feel nervous.

She was a *switch* Switch who had recognised him, and knew who Miranda was. That was very worrying. He briefly wondered what web-page his family was starring on.

'Henry, can I see your chest?' Arthur asked, 'I need a little bit of reassuring.'

'Only if I can see your ankle.' Henry replied.

Henry's chest was welts of fish. It was the worry that was making the welts, and his imagination making them into fish. Arthur nodded, relieved. Henry had been behaving too strangely for himself, but now he had seen his chest, he felt better. It was probably the worry of the new happenings that was making him so stupid.

If you *talk* Switch, Switch will react. Maybe Henry's conscience was conveniently making him forgetful about that now. Arthur had never heard him ever say sorry about past curses, but he would eventually make excuses for starting them. Today he was shocked a Switch would ever take him seriously, but yesterday he would have been mortally offended if they had took no notice at all.

Henry had never cursed family before. His guilt complex must be working at twice the speed to make him behave so innocently, so quickly.

Henry nodded at Arthur's feet. 'Your turn.'

Arthur nodded, and rolled down his sock.

More fish.

They were cartoon fish that were made out of the lines of the dented skin that had been created by Arthur's socks. They were not realistic because Arthur was standing too close to the lakeside.

Arthur didn't want the fish to think they could breathe air, float in air, stick to his ankle, or, do anything else that was impossible for fish to do.

He liked fish. They had a slight connection with Henry and Arthur because of their colouring. The fish in the lake had subtle human, facial looking dark splodges on their skin. It was like a black and white photo of a human face was on the trunk of their body.

They were skin – talkers, like the tube dwellers, and themselves.

They were very good at bodily insinuating. One movement of the fin, and they would subtly raise an eyebrow of the face on their back. A movement in the tail, and the splodges would turn into a sneer. Their trunk faces were permanent, unlike witches, but they were less obvious in their feelings. They were very subtle sneerers. If you need a best friend that doesn't blurt, have a fish, not a witch.

Some cats were the same as the fish, or near enough as they could be. Arthur had cats. His cats were black and white, and had the same face type pattern on their fur. With his cats, it was like half a face rather than the whole one. He imagined they used to be full head type shadows on their fur, but that they had changed it to something less grabbed - they were probably mistaken for fancy dress masks centuries before.

His study was black and white. A fake splodgy black and white cow rug was on the ground and an armchair was covered in the same fake black and white pattern. He let the cats hide in there, and it amazed him, sometimes, how easily they blended in.

Some dogs too, had the same colouring. He had thought of buying a Dalmatian dog, but worried it might get upset at the faux cow rug. They were quite similar.

The cats spent their time looking for mirrors so they could make a whole face. He had also noticed that they practised moving their limbs in front of the mirror, so that their face pattern would look sympathetic when anyone started moaning about their day.

The reason cat owners started stroking their cats is because they didn't like the cat's body pulling faces at them when they were talking, Arthur thought. They were holding them still. He had noted his own cats smirked, sulked, raised eyebrows and looked sad, all with the same fur pattern and a gentle manipulation of muscles.

Cows would probably do the same, if they had large enough mirrors. Instead the patterned ones always put themselves in strategic places in the herd, so they could astound hand gliders with a giant face, as seen from above. They only needed three of themselves, that were splodgy, to make eyes and a mouth.

Occasionally a calf would be used as a tongue, to run out from under the mouth cow, as if waiting for the hand glider to fall in.

It was as if to say, 'What would you do if it was the other way round?'

Cows were quite like spiders, in some ways.

Fish are a lot easier to observe than cows, as Arthur didn't need a hand glider to do it.

Fish, cows, dogs, cats.... Any animal that has markings are precious to some of the skin-talking people, who think that they are particularly intelligent animals, and should be treated as such. It is, they say, unethical to eat a creature who has gone to so much trouble to tell you not to.

Most train-dwellers, who didn't actually live on tube trains, but used them to get around, and witches, were vegetarians, because animals had mouths, eyes, ears limbs and everything else they identified with. It wasn't just a skin-thing- but the skin-thing helped.

Even though the skin talkers normally did not have naked

meetings anymore, they did occasionally have get togethers to see what their skins were saying. Spying on them may look as if they were acting out a sex position guidebook, but some of the skin pictorials really have to be looked at closely to see what they are.

Arthur and Henry's welts looked like tabby cat tiger stripes, too.

They tried to please all possible observers, all of the time, and they were in a wooded, and perhaps inhabited, area.

They made a sort of synchronised, half-hearted 'ya' sound to show their recognised similarity, and leaned back further against the tree. It sheltered them from the rain.

Arthur looked up. He had only just noticed. The rain was glittering. It was multi coloured. He held out his hand to catch some in his palm.
It was another new.
He shuddered, waiting for the chain reaction of newness to develop into chain reactions of opened potato bag and no-oiled swing proportions.

The cult leader had reached the village without another spontaneous outbreak of verbal communication with herself. It had been difficult to park. Not because of the people, but because there were no car parks. She had, in the end, left the car ten minutes away, in a supermarket car park, and walked.
Walking didn't bother her. She had had another minor embarrassment with the shop window, when she had asked herself 'why blue shoes? ' but the walk was eventless, apart from that.
She sighed.

She'll have breakfast first. On her own.

The village was just over a road, and through a sheltered path. She had been there once before, while looking for a person who had once appeared in a newspaper report. It had been a pointless journey, but she had found a little café there that she could go to, should she ever return. Fame used to be a commodity, and she had wanted some of it for a Switch. They would pay good money to have a bit of the fame a newspaper report would bring.

The problem with England that it was so small, that it was like one of those driving nightmares where you drive and drive but never get anywhere but back at the beginning again. It looked big enough to get lost in, but wasn't.

That is how the cult leader felt.

The village was packed already.

News travelled fast in a small place.

Her eyes skimmed the crowd, looking for a Myra, to reflect herself, or a Miranda.

She missed her own face in a crowd.

The covens she was part of wore hoods, to disguise the member's features. As each person represented a 'face' this was thought a wise thing to do. That face might represent a hundred or more of the same face, and the coven leaders didn't want any squabbles among the Switches.

None they hadn't organised themselves.

If other coven members saw which face another Switch was representing they may kill the twin faces prematurely. 'Cull' wasn't a word she liked to use, but it happened frequently. Those that were in the spotlight of the TV and media soon found that the greed and envy of others ridded themselves of doppelgangers, before they disappeared themselves. She wouldn't like a coven member to suddenly find themselves without a face to turn into two.

She, of course, knew all the faces. She was allowed to see them, individually, without a hood.

There was one or two of her coven faces, in the crowd. If they sent their leader to her coven, they should recognise her, from photos, and make her feel welcome, but only if they felt their own faces had been accepted as local people.

She was beautiful. Everyone looked at her anyway, so nobody was suspicious when she was the centre of attention. She wore jewellery, in a pre-arranged sequence, to identify her from other beautiful twins. The jewellery was individual and not easily purchased. Of course, it was sold to wannabe's, after it was no use to her anymore. She could only wear it once or twice, before other twins would try to be her.

She sold the jewellery at auctions. It always sold for far more than it was worth, because of her status in the coven, and it financed other pieces of jewellery to be made. And left enough over, to support her lifestyle.

They thought they could use it to command her covens, she supposed.

No one recognised her yet, so no one was there. All their attention was on the sky.

A cloud was forming, and they seemed particularly engrossed by it. So much so that they hadn't noticed she wasn't wearing grey, like they all were. No-one had even looked in her direction, and she *was* beautiful.

She glimpsed at the sky. The mouse spoon was disappearing, and it was starting to rain. It was a pleasant sight, but not one that was worth making an effort for. The sun shone with a rainbow,

turning the rain a sparkly stream of colour.
The cloud forming was changing. Two little humps, like eyebrows appeared.

The cult leader turned away and looked for the little café that she had found before.

It is hard to believe that Mrs. Lock and the cult leader were unaware of each others presence and habits, as their timing was perfected to just managing to avoid each other.

It was like the same event happened every year.

Mrs. Lock walked straight ahead, and a gap in the crowd opened to let her in, and just as silently closed again. The people were all taller and wider than she was, so she was easily disguised as one of them. The cult leader turned left, to enter the café door, as the last glimpse of Mrs. Lock's coat disappeared from view. They were less than three feet apart.
Miranda watched, stunned.
Mrs. Lock had given her one last look at her skin, as she was pocketing the individual sugar portions.
Her face had become younger as she sorted brown sugar packets from white sugar packets.
Her forehead had stopped wrinkling, and the lines around her eyes cleared. It was if Miranda had seen the effects of Botox injections, speeded up.
Her jowls also disappeared and her eyes lost the blood shot look.
The age spots disappeared.
She was young.
Miranda stared at Mrs. Lock's hair, expecting it to change colour, but it stayed the same grey-blond it was before.

A glazed look had appeared in Mrs. Lock's eyes as she rose and left.

Just before she turned away Miranda saw eyes appear on her forehead. They were as real looking as a flesh coloured sculpture. They looked at her and blinked.

Then she was gone through the door, and into the crowd outside.

Miranda thought for a second that she had turned around and come back in, but the clothes weren't similar. And the woman at the door was beautiful.

The woman at the door was staring at her

Chapter 6

Switches happen quickly, normally after an argument, if the person being switched is not a Switch.

The coven leader was hoping that Henry would still be angry. Anger makes people oblivious to small changes in a loved one, but doesn't last long. If she could get rid of Miranda, and put her own Miranda in her place, while he was still annoyed, then he might not notice the new Miranda trying to find her way to her own bedroom. The Miranda double could blame the quarrel as an excuse for any behavioural change that he notices in her, too.

They couldn't get close to Miranda when she was young, which was a pity. Children are gullible. But they had tried. If only she wasn't so… verbal… she would have listened to their eyes more.

The Coven leader wasn't really concerned about where Miranda would go. She was never really concerned about where the natural child went.

If she had been a younger child, then they would have probably kept the child somewhere, ready to swap. That is how their cult grew. Displace and command. As long as they were all cult children, she didn't mind. She could walk into any house and demand obedience and possessions. She was known as a saviour, rather than kidnapper. Sometimes, for fun, and if she particularly disliked a family, she would sell the natural child their own inheritance back, at twice it's value. Sentimentality was profitable.

Most of the time they were made to rent their own deceased relatives property, unaware that it was theirs anyway, so she could live off the proceeds.

Her and her chosen faces.

She had expenses to pay, but still…

The families she didn't like were the ones like the witches, who didn't let her in or recognise her importance.

Even though Miranda had escaped their attention in childhood, at least one of them would be there in her teenage years.

It wasn't particularly important if they couldn't persuade her. There were plenty of people naïve enough to let the Switch inside their lifestyle, it's just that the witches were reputed to be wealthier than most families. Witches did not share their possessions with look-a-likes, so had more of everything. They did not believe in common wealth. That meant to them, that one did the work, while the others profited from that work, without contributing. That is why the cult leader did not like them. They were right. She lived off the hard work that others did.

Of course, Witches didn't have the confusion and upset that unrelated twins bought with them, so they were a bit meaner with strangers.

But they sometimes gave birth to children like Miranda. Swappable.

She looked at Miranda with hidden dislike.

'Can you help me?' She asked. 'My name is..' she thought of a suitable name. One that fitted her present emotion, so she would not forget this person, or this place. A name usually gave her a clue, when she re visited, to whether she liked being there. When she visited the town next to the village, she had left the name Mrs. May, because she may like to visit again. To a potential boyfriend she would be, perhaps, 'Cally' so she would remember to call.

Other people were her walking memo's.

To Miranda, she would be Violet. She felt violent towards her. 'My name is Violet. I am a newspaper reporter. Could you tell me what's happening here?'

She sat herself opposite Miranda and smiled politely.

120

The texts had said about Henry's impromptu announcement, and another about the sky changing. She knew why they were outside, but Miranda didn't, else she would have been outside too, watching the most important event of the last couple of decades.

Violet hadn't made plans to be in the village to see the weather change. Seeing it rain just didn't register as an important occasion for her. She had never believed the rumours or any newspaper reports she had been shown, but had hinted at children that if it did happen, then *she* was the one that had *made* it happen. It was such a small thing really, but pretending to have influence with those that controlled the weather gave her credence in other areas of her life. She had never believed the sky was natural. She had always given credit to the military.

She endeavoured to be the first person a baby heard the cloud stories from too, so she could claim that she put them there. Babies never forgot their first influences. They would remember her later, and pay her respect, then money...

If it was happening outside, then she would have a tape of it. She didn't need to be out in the rain herself.

Violet would let Miranda answer first, and then she would know if she was Henry's grandchild, or one of theirs.

She could surprise her with a little hint of what was purportedly happening outside, if she didn't know.

It was always best to look like a giver, when in reality, she was a taker.

The crowds outside smiled at Mrs. Lock. She was thirty years old, naturally, and without her look-down-at-herself and light induced wrinkles, she looked younger.

The crowd knew her better than herself, they thought. Well, they knew her appearance better than she did herself.

They slowly bought out their cameras and opened a path for her to walk through.

Some of the cameras were discreet, but mostly they had giant zoom lenses on them. They were all aimed at Mrs. Locks exposed skin; her face, hands, and neck, and at the sky.

Arthur jumped when his mobile phone made a sound.

Him and Henry were engrossed with sky watching. The rainy clouds were morphing. Two eyebrows appeared, followed by two eyes. It gave the appearance that a head was beginning to look up from a chest. The length of the nose was beginning to appear.

Henry had trained his mobile on the sight.

'Arthur, I don't believe we forgot about this.'

'I know, Henry, I know. 'He replied, turning his own phone off. The noise had been a text from Rene, asking for help at the shop.

Clouds had always been the objects of inspiration and whimsical stories. They were the basis of most myths and most TV story lines. They played an important part in a region's history and rituals. The witches had their legend in the sky, as did the Switches and the normal people.

The stories were always the same plots because the clouds always appeared in the same sequence. It is the sequence that people wanted to remember. They needed to remember the sequence because of the vegetable farming they did. Rain was coming, or not coming. Floods were imminent or not imminent. Drought periods were noted.

The head profiles in the sky were hailed as heroes or villains, in the story telling, depending on whether they appeared in the sky before or after a dark clouded storm, or whether they were between periods of strong sun light.

The stories were never meant to apply to the people who resembled the clouds, but eventually did, as the characters of some changed to what they thought they were hearing about themselves.

It seemed that Switches and others were more susceptible to being the legends than those that actually worked in the community.

Vegetable farmers tended to know what the stories were for, so kept their own minds.

The sky had always been the same.
Ever since anyone could remember.

Then Mrs. Lock was born and the sky, for ten seconds, changed. People ideas changed. Opinions changed. It changed the world.

Then everyone forgot, except a few.

No one who was a witness could decide whether the sky changed first or whether Mrs. Lock had been born first. Mrs. Lock was never asked, but if she had been asked, while she had still remembered, she would have said the sky had changed first. She had felt like she had been born on someone else's famous birthday, and that she looked exactly like that person, but without their prestige. She had also felt like she should have cheered herself, before instantly being embarrassed that she could have thought she could have ever been her doppelganger. That she felt, was the usual birth.

The sky, and her, had been mentioned in the newspapers, for a while, in reports that emphasized the similarity people seemed to be gaining towards the clouds. They were beginning to resemble the cloud heads, in the sky, apparently more and more each year. Mrs. Lock was proof of their influence. The newspapers blamed new technology and a thing called the 'ozone' layer.

The purist Switches, still hiding their heads from each other, and the non-switching twins, who were just as sensitive, gained sympathy and public support at their sentiments; that they did become what they see, they all agreed. They held up little banners and big hand-shaped cardboard cut outs on sticks, which pointed at the sky, to prove they had spent a lot of time thinking about it.

More people stopped looking at the sky, and avoided the tube dwellers, along with keeping away from people with interesting profiles. Instead they concentrated on advertising posters and cinema stars. The film stars spoke, said the normal people, so would encourage the unborn to speak later. And the film stars had arms and legs, unlike cloud formations.

Their genes would be saved by buying a ticket to the afternoon matinee.

Some of them suggested starting a war, or using coal in the fire places, so the clouds would turn into fog or at least be hidden by billowing smoke, but that would have been being hysterical and silly.

Mrs. Lock being born was proof for the purists. She was covered in the sky, with figures, faces, letters and numbers.
When the sky changed, her skin changed to match.
It cleared, and aped what she could not see too, which were her thoughts.

Not just one patch, like most skin-talkers, but all over, all of the time.

Thirty years ago, she had been born. It had been in October. Just after the Mouse Cloud turned into the Spoon Cloud, it became Spoon Head Cloud.
'And the mouse looked into the spoon,' some said, 'and reflected it's image on earth. '

'Human was born of mouse-head-spoon reflection.'

The newspapers had said the sky phenomenon had been caused by a bout of high pressure meeting low. It was, said their experts, a narrowly avoided hurricane or typhoon.

And some people said other things, like; the face that half-appeared with the spectacular rain was just Mrs. Locks.

A legend had been born, as proof of the god's existence.

The sky was x-rays of the people beneath, and their godly status.

 Mrs. Lock was born to gather her ancestor's harvest, the heaven and the earth, they claimed. But she was far too young to go harvesting at her ancestors, so they would gather it for her.

Henry had forgotten the interest that the baby face had been surrounded by. He had had photos of her, just as all the skin talkers had. The first photo of her had been photos of her head, with the similar expected- unexpected, images that the clouds had just made.

There had been two eyes, with brows, looking down on her own baby eye brows. They were coloured with a skin tone slightly darker than the babies own. If he hadn't known, he would think an artist was using her as canvas.

Henry had wondered if other images on her face had meant to show wind direction, or the area where the high pressure had come from.

The baby had the skin of a weather caster, or at least, the skin of the map next to the weather-caster.

Her skin had shown the sky above, but had also showed a weather front moving in over her neck. She had been predicting, he presumed

He looked down at his chest.
'Arthur, those welts on your leg; they are not tidal waves are they?
Arthur frowned. 'Why?'
'Baby X. The baby extraordinaire. She showed hell and damnation on her skin. Do you remember that photo? I kept that photo when I sold the collection. Hell and damnation is normally accompanied by Tsunamis, and that is what my chest looks like. Look – there's even a little tiny ship. Aww –isn't it cute?'
Arthur nodded slowly. He hadn't thought of Baby X since it had happened. He had been in his teens. They used to play swaps-it with the photos that were released. Arthur was more interested in the newspaper report that had accompanied the photo. They had been told to remember it, and they had forgotten. It warned that unless environmental issues were resolved the high pressure would return. The scientific calculations said it would be exactly

thirty years before the face would be back in the sky, if habits were not changed. Whether or not the high pressure would cause hurricanes and tidal waves in the future, they didn't know. It was likely, if the aberration returned.

Arthur slowly realised what Henry was hinting at. He looked at his leg.

'We are baby X?'

Newspapers hardly ever used real photos of people involved in a story; else they would be accused of being cult-leaders, leading the cull. Photos were stock photos.

Arthur reddened. He had never thought baby X was himself or Henry. He hadn't thought it was any of the skin talkers. They had tried to find baby X though, and wasn't able to. Maybe it was because she didn't exist.

Henry was already phoning Eileen, and staring at the sky again. He motioned to Arthur to take photos of the clouds.

Arthur turned his mobile phone back on. He was a prophet, and he didn't know it.

Graham's mum had been busy talking to the window, when she heard the door shut.

Graham had stared at the part of the glass that was misting up, before he had left. He had drawn a smiley face on the window for her to talk to.

In the past, he had wondered if his mum was trying to communicate with the clouds. The clouds were a local pre occupation. She told the time by those clouds. She could tell which day in which month it was by looking at those clouds. They were mostly face shaped or in a recognisable arrangement.

The villagers had spent years guessing if they spelt out a pictogram message, as they changed from one cloud formation to another in rapid succession.

They were English clouds, they had decided.

The pictogram message only made sense in English, and English rhyming words.

The face ones looked like his relatives.

One of them, which would appear in a week's time, was like his Uncle George.

THE WEATHER; It is not a well known fact to weather reporters that it is the land that moves, not the sky. Clouds moving, while the land stays still, are frequently shown on the television, just after the news, broadcasting the weather. They don't even get the weather person to wobble the map anymore, just to show that *they know*.

People who know that the land moves avoid mentioning it directly, because no one else does. Anyway, it seems to imply, they think, that they are self - destructive in living on a planet that chases hurricanes and other bad weather fronts.

CLOUDS; the clouds the weather makes are important in some social groups, as the cloud formations are very repetitive.

The same shapes appear year after year, and unless you are familiar to an area you would not know which cloud formation happens next. This, it is thought, protects the natives of a town from strangers.

128

Some of the social groups use the clouds as a code for gossip, a memory aid for weather forecasting, and repetitive bad events. For example, a woman might say, 'Ermantrude, (her - man-intrude), is going through a passage to talk to Albert (Her, but) but she is about to fall into the gutter.'

This could mean the resembling passing clouds will be followed by an enormous storm, so they have enough time to go somewhere safe.

Or it could mean that cousin Alberta is a nutter, who has pushed cousin Ermantrude in to a gutter, but knows the power lines will be down because of the weather, so won't be caught.

It may be a regular event too, but to say it in normal English could mean that the gossips might be seen as co conspirators towards Ermantrude's actual bodily harm.

Betrayal of forming cloud patterns, and their connection with local events, was sometimes used as a private, illegal way of making money. The weather gossip could be used by a stranger to imply they were local or the weather pattern may be used for a cover for a stranger's crimes.

If an angled mirror is found in a bedroom, showing clouds, in it's reflection, it may mean the owner of it will want payment for telling stories of the clouds... you know... the.. erm.. *clouds* .

The bedroom is high enough to reflect the clouds.

The mirror was usually round and angled to show a profile of a cloud shaped as a face. (The mirror was also supposed to look like a giant coin.)

The reflected cloud profile would be the subject of a gossipy conversation about a similar local person, – their wealth, their reputation and marital status, but would be hidden under the guise of a story created for the weather pattern.

The people who charged for telling local secrets were shunned and disliked by the community. After the first betrayals the 'Ors', as they were called, were only told lies by the locals, to sell on.

These lies were known as 'tall tales', because the locals looked up, at bedroom windows as they passed by, knowing what was said in that bedroom were lies.

The word 'Or' was made from the shape of a tilted, oval mirror on a stand.

Many old portrait paintings had the cloud-angled mirror included, as a guide to the person's character or for the date. (The passing cloud formations, in each area, had been made into fairy stories of good or bad. The mirror would reflect a cloud appropriate to the person.)

A poem by Tennyson – 'The Lady of Shallot' is thought to be about a woman who hears about her own reputation through a mirror sky-er. A mirror sky-er is the name given to someone who uses the clouds to give Switches an idea of what their twins are like. (A scryer is a modern way of spelling it.)

The lady of Shallot is told that her reflection sits in a river because the woman she resembled, who resembled a cloud, was thundery and destructive, but then passed away. The woman is told it like a fairy story of herself, so she will not become offended but will repeat it, and unintentionally warn others of her character, without becoming violent to the story-teller.

The sky-er is not an Or.

Graham's mother stared at the groups of people accumulating on the hill, and carried on chatting to herself.

She was told never to look alone if there was only a piece of glass to separate her from a would-be-Switch.

There was usually one or two that subconsciously kept her mouth busy, but today there were hundreds of them, so she was talking non-stop.

She would have bought a dog to chat to, but from the window it may seem like she was talking to a child. She didn't want her house to be a Switch house after she was gone, with years of non-aging children passing through. They mirrored what they saw. Forever.

Talking to cats made it look as if she was talking to the window, or even worse, the pot on the cooker.

Standing near the cooking ring used to be a favourite with some cats, because it was slightly warm. She didn't want to make it look as if she was chatting to her food, so didn't have cats.

She looked up and realised.

Something was different.

Not just the people, but the rain.

She stopped talking and closed the curtains.

That was better.

She wondered why she had never done that before. Closing the curtains is a remedy. Now she would just have to have a lava lamp in the middle of the room, so the shadows of it showed through the curtains. That would be 'other-people-are-here-too' like. She could stop talking to herself.

Grahams mum pulled on her shoes.
She had a sudden urge to see the sky.

SOCK PORTRAITS; sociologists have studied the dust patterns on plain socks for a very long time. It is the little pattern of black dots on white sport socks that they have

found particularly interesting. They said it showed how orderly the wearer's mind was. It was the spacing of the black dots, and the arrangement of them, that made good watching. It was amazing, they added, that some were very similar to star constellations, when space exploration was popular.
The sociologists did not see anything wrong with zooming gym changing rooms with hidden cameras.
They weren't sex pests or sock sniffers.

Honestly.

The sky eyes, she thought, looked like two sock ends, seen from beneath. The eye brows were the sock tops. The rain was the washing machine water running from them.

.

As some people could hardly remember the first appearance of the October Eyes head, it's characteristics were frequently argued about.

The argument was mostly about the size of its nose. Whether it was small, large, bent or straight. It was important to some people, who believed in gods, to whom the face belonged to. The face it belonged to would rule the world, when it re appeared. It was, in the retelling, the head of a god.
The nose was first,
The nose was all,
It was the nose
That made the world a ball.
The nose people had mistaken sneezes as the wind, Miranda had thought. Those people's lives depended on the shape of their

noses. Miranda had noticed the same with her mother. A two inch by a two inch square piece of skin and connective tissue had dictated her whole life to her. She bonded with other noses. Her mole, just as important, was her other lifestyle choice. She could only see the two ways of living. The nasal people were very narrow minded.

Another story was the cloud mouth would speak, when it appeared. It didn't the first time.

The shape of the mouth of the cloud was also argued about, but less loudly. The mouth people wanted people to see the shapes of their mouths, so didn't move it much. They sort of argued out of the corner of their lips.
The clouds were their truth… because they had tooths.
They would have used their eyes to talk with, but wanted other people to notice their mouths. Their mouths were their most prominent feature.
They used a lot of lip salve and lipstick when putting their point of view across.
There had been a rise in birth rates, for a while, as everyone tried to produce the predicted sky god's features. Mouth people mixed with nose people, and nose people mixed with small eared people. There were no ears to the face, they had heard.
Together they thought they would make at least one person who resembled the next god.

But that was the people who were still tribal, and thought that if they ignored the invention of trains, the euro tunnel, planes and ferries, and time generally moving forwards, overseas visitors would as well. And then they would stop coming here.
Without the visitors the tribalists could re-establish mud huts, grass skirts, and worshipping.

They would be alone again with their savage lifestyle.
They would pick one of themselves to be god, if *their* image was in the sky, even if modern day people wouldn't.

☼

Most people who were crowding the village knew the face in the sky was similar to Mrs. Locks.
They had accumulated to see her.
They knew she would be there. They had followed her.

☼

Mrs. Lock took another step. A nose appeared, exactly the same as hers, on her forehead, beneath the skin eyes. The nose was a little nose, but slightly lopsided. It was a nose that was rare.
As the same appeared on the cloud above, a loud groan erupted from some of the crowd, masked by cheers that were just as loud.
The sudden sounds startled Mrs. Lock out of her somnambulance.
She still couldn't quite remember why she was standing in a crowd of people, or why she felt that she should walk up the path they had created for her, but she did.
The crowd waited with suspense to see the shape of the mouth.

Mobile phones silently exchanged photos and business cards with 'Photo Shop alterations at the Best Prices' were discreetly handed out to those that looked disappointed.
.

☼

Graham was standing to one side of the hill, behind his house. The crowd seemed to have thickened, but not with people wearing grey. Grey clothing hadn't normally been a popular

134

colour since homosexual people adopted the word 'gay' to describe their sexual preference. Some thought they just didn't want heterosexuals to be happy, so had tried to stop them using the word 'gay' to describe their mood.

Homosexuals were the gayest, -the happiest- and heterosexuals weren't allowed to be anymore, they conveyed.

No-one knows who adopted the term. It was supposed that the homosexuals that were unhappy about being homosexual thought that they would be more contented using a word that describes 'happy' rather than using a four syllable word that can't be mistaken for any another synonym.

The people he had noticed from the house window were obviously not gay, but grey. The clothing was smartly ironed shades of grey with white shirts or blouses.

The newcomers were a faded mixture of the other colours, and mostly in jeans and coats. They were *definitely* not in *gay* colours, or *grey* colours or any colours that implied gayness. They were wearing *faded.*

He shuffled nearer the front. The greys were a mixture of sizes and shapes.

There were several giants, trying to look at ease while balancing on a lower angle, so they seemed shorter.

It had worked. Graham hadn't noticed them at a distance. There were dwarves too, and elfin type figures. The elfins were too short to be giants, but too tall to be average. They were standing on a different slope. They were thin, naturally. Of course, there were lots of people like him too.

He followed their eyes and cameras to the sky. Some of them… well, most of them had two cameras. One pointed to the sky, and another to the empty path they had spontaneously made from parting the crowd.

The sky was particularly interesting today, he supposed. Worth filming. He couldn't remember seeing the clouds arranged like that before. The sun was still shining, and the rainbow was still curving, while the rain still rained.

There was a head rising out of the clouds. It seemed to be in the process of looking up from a chest. As he had watched it had developed a nose, which had followed the eyes.

The man in front of him, who was holding his camera high in front of Graham's view of the clouds, was slightly shaking.

Graham shrugged and pulled out his camera. It must be an important cloud, and film worthy.

'No' Miranda replied to the coven leader. She did not know what was happening outside, and she did not know where Mrs. Lock had gone either. She was just about to buy her some yeast-free, sugar-free, wheat-free biscuits too.

But her face had changed. She hadn't looked starving anymore. She looked … young but her eyes looked.. dozy. The skin eyes, on her forehead, had been scarily real.

'Why don't you go and have a look? I am.' Miranda added as the woman calling herself Violet took Mrs.Locks seat.

She saw, see saw, Miranda thought as she stood up, as Violet had sat down. She didn't like the look of Violet. Perhaps it was because she was thinking of Mrs. Lock's eyes, but Violets looked tiny and nasty in comparison.

'You can have this table, 'she added, in case Violet was thinking that she was inviting her to go with her.

Then she followed Mrs. Lock out of the doorway.

Miranda wasn't particularly interested in the assorted group. She had been to festivals before. She had also witnessed trains having to stop in weird places, because of the weather.

The unexpected rain had probably halted the day's timetable, leaving the passengers stranded.

Miranda looked around her. The path that had opened up for Mrs Lock had gone, and Miranda had been left looking at broad shoulders. She glanced behind her at the café.
Strangely, a childhood rhyme came into her head. 'A day will come when you will fall, because all that you heard, will herd you all.' She was looking in the café window, searching for Mrs. Lock's reflection, when she thought of that. The group were quite like a herd, she supposed. But herds don't go grey. She had never seen animals – big animals - go grey. She didn't know if elephants were always *grey*, or if they only let stray film crews follow them home when they reached old age.
Grey wasn't a natural colour in scenery either.

The grey clothed group were mingled with other less particularly dressed people.

In the quick glimpse that she had, she noticed two things.
One was Mrs. Lock just ahead. She had seen the back of her coat reflected in the glass. It was a distinctive green colour. She was about a hundred or so foot ahead.
Another thing she noticed, almost subliminally, was the multicoloured faded cloth people seemed to be stalking, in pairs.

As if the grey crowd *were* cattle. There was a person behind and to the side of the tallest. It was the sort of positioning that farmers took, shown on the telly, when a quadruped was being walked.

They were mostly Switches, she was almost certain.

She pushed past the most obvious of the Switches, and tried to catch up with Mrs. Lock.

Chapter 7

Violet, as she had called herself, turned a scarlet colour. She was embarrassed. People did not walk away from her.

Perhaps Miranda was colour coordinating her thoughts. She had predicted that Violet would go red, after being violet. Who wouldn't go red, after being so blatantly snubbed?
Violet objected to being part of Miranda's thought projection. She was being namist. And she also objected to the messy table.
Empty biscuit packets were scattered and a half eaten pasta dish was on the plate near the place her elbows were resting.
There was a half drunken glass of water, and opposite, where Miranda had been sitting, a plate of crumbling mushrooms.
Violet wasn't a rubbish-reader. She left that to the tramps. They would dissect clutter into a cohesive thought pattern with a quick look and 'learn psychology–in-ten-steps.' book. They were mostly wrong, but it let Violet know how, and what, they were like themselves.

She moved to another table, and ordered a coffee.

Skin talkers, witches and Switches had been called lots of things over the centuries.

One name was Stupid.

There was no point in staring at the back of a person and hoping they would notice that you were asking for a bowl of

chips, just because you had a bowl of chips icon on your forehead. That was Stupid. Lots of skin talkers did exactly that sort of thing, and lots of eye-talkers did nearly exactly the same stupid thing by trying to talk with their eyes.

Another name-calling term had been 'Fish'.

Fish had no discernable, distinguishable ears, had pointy heads, and bulgy eyes. Switches, skin talkers and witches were compared to them because of their fondness for triangular hats and not using their mouths to communicate with.

Switches also said 'don't know', with their eyes a lot too. It looked like they were saying 'no-nose.' Fish didn't have noses. Some people think fish evolved to what they thought people looked like; as if they overheard a common description but had never seen a human themselves.

Their no 'no-nose' stance also implied to a lot of people that they were actually saying 'skull' when their eyes hovered around the nasal area.
Nostrils look similar to a no-jawed skull… and you know that piece of skin under the nose? The philtrum? That looked like some kind of pole holding the skull up.
Unexplained nose-communication was thought have planted a seed of thought that caused a whole lot of domino effect disasters, including the regime of Pol-pot who was thought to have placed lots of heads on sticks. Pol-pot didn't have a philtrum. Some people think him not having a philtrum was the direct cause of his skull on sticks fetish; thinking that when the soon-to-be- dead people tried to say 'no', by just using their eyes, he thought they were mocking his lack of nasal area, resulting in an inflamed temper and his 'how-do-

you like it' attitude.

Early drawings of fish, that depicted the skin-talking witches, had had darker patches of scales drawn on them, around the neck area, that hinted at the colour gold. Hoping that the people who saw the drawings could rhyme, it was meant as a warning that the fish people said they were already old, to any area, and would kill for gold, kill the old, and do anything else that sounded like the word 'collar' and the word 'gold'.

There were two reasons that skin talkers, witches and switches were reputedly dunked into water occasionally. One was to extinguish their 'flame-like' skin, - that was for skin talkers - the other was because all of them were categorised as 'fish' on a tick-list of what a fish is. Fish presumably needed water, and most people are obliging to needs.

Eileen's skin wasn't a skin talkers skin. It was more of a skin-mumbling type of skin. Her blood rose to the surface in commutative spots.
She had been accepted as a Switch, because they had said her skin condition was eczema. They also said it was acne, and psoriasis.
It depended on who was looking, she supposed, and how they saw things.

She wasn't as picturesque as Henry.
Sometimes she envied him his easy images.

She was walking the back way, to the café, stopping to lean on trees, to have a little sleep, and to look at the sky. A mouth was appearing, made of clouds.

She was too tired to join the crowds. Besides, she had to get to Miranda before something bad happened.

To know the Switches were still watching, even after all these years, was unbearable. She hadn't exactly left their groupings, but had avoided the people she knew were them. It was hard to know who was a Switch, though, because they would be Switched even after they had been Switched. No one wanted to be nasty to an innocent Switch. That was like booing a baby monkey who had been put in a cage with monkey-tearing apes. One day she might be that baby monkey, and she might look round and find her friends were strangers.
No, the best thing was to be aloof but pleasant.

She thought Mrs. Lock was there because she was a Switch, and was there for revenge. She couldn't think of any other reason she would be sitting with Miranda.

She had tried talking to Mrs. Lock once.

Mrs. Lock had replied and Eileen had instinctively accused her, silently, of echoing her, which was a stupid thing to do. Eileen had been taught to accuse others of her own bad behaviour at the first chance she got and the disapproval in Eileen's eyes had turned Mrs. Lock's eyes away.
Then she had stalked her for a while, until Mrs.Lock had become too famous.
It was so sad. She had heard rumours of Mrs.Locks amnesia so she had tried again. The next time she approached Mrs. Lock she had smiled at her. Mrs. Lock had smiled too, and had said hello. The conversation had died out. It had lasted about twenty seconds. It was Mrs. Locks fault, thought Eileen. Mrs. Lock didn't use her eyes to talk with and Eileen didn't feel like she

142

could stand there and stare at her skin. Mrs. Lock was looking at her too openly for her to study her. She had probably wanted more verbal communication. Some people felt that they could only make themselves clear by verbal communication, and she was one of those types.

Eileen could see her point. Some of them, that used just their skin, or just their eyes, seemed a bit dim.

It was mostly because they missed some of the conversation.

It was difficult to listen to more than one person when it was the skin that was talking.

Skin talking was more for intimate chat, rather than for crowds or slight friends. A moving hemline could change the whole meaning of a sentence.

It was kind of like cloud watching. One person may point out a cloud face, and by the time the companion looks, that bit of cloud has changed into something else.

Eileen didn't use her skin often, to talk with. Her skin didn't really make her meaning clear. She used her eyes and voice too.

Sometimes her skin sort of erupted with spots when she tried to say something with them.

She would be thinking she had said something clearly and concisely, without moving her eyes, but the person opposite would be just wondering why she didn't use a good face cream once in a while.

They just didn't look close enough. Her spots, when they appeared, were rhyming spots. When two appeared, it could mean 'do ', or 'shoe' or 'loo'. Anything that rhymed with a number.

She got acne when she was hungry. Her skin would rhyme 'hungry' with hundred spots, all at once, with three separate spots a few centimetres away. 'hun-three' it pictured at people.

She imagines she tried to stay hungry, so her subconscious couldn't be read so easily. Other number spots got lost in the heap of hungry spots.

Eileen really over exaggerated her skins talking abilities.

Some couldn't help their skin talking for them. It did it's own thing as well as communicating thoughts. Mrs. Lock's did that. You had to know her well to know what she was actually thinking, and what was on her skin already.
Eileen's Community group studied her for ages before they knew the difference.
Her skin sometimes went into a loop of chattiness about evolution, in the hope it would distract, confuse or entertain anyone within a foot of her, while she was actually thinking of something completely different, and while a sky-scape lingered on her forehead.

Mrs Lock's skin also changed to what was in front of her.

Eileen had seen others the same. Their skin was an enthusiastic miniature mirror of what they had just seen. Normally in caricature form. It could be embarrassing for them, especially if they were trying to be tactful.
She never got too close to people like them. Mrs. Lock was different. She was just One.
The people she was thinking of were more groupy. They were sensitive and normally dressed in white, with white head coverings, so they could look at themselves and each other without reflecting. They wore veils when they could. If they only looked at white, their skin would clear for a bit.
Their clothes, being white, showed every speckle of tomato sauce or every flick of mashed potato.
They normally appeared at festivals and things like that so they could look disapprovingly at anyone that was eating take away food.

They liked people to notice the whiteness of their clothes, and the reason they wore white.

If they stayed in, nobody would know how special they were.

Also, even though their laundry bill was expensive it was better than their skin being sarcastic about their friends or about someone bigger than they were, they thought.

That could cause worse incidents.

She looked around her worriedly, in case they were in the village too.

Her skin might be showing cafeteria intentions, and that would irritate them.

She couldn't see any whiter-than-white clothing in the growing crowd but the crowd was reaching pre-festival proportions and that was just as worrying.

Eileen had a quick look for tie-dyed sheets spread out on the pavement, loaded with faux opals and clay on a string, but luckily, there wasn't as many people as there seemed. If there was, they would be there, crossed legged, trying to sell fakes to fakes. The path was clear of charlatans. Not even a one-pavement-slab candle seller.

She always looked for them when she was in a crowd, hoping that one day she would find a real stone seller. A real stone seller sold natural pebbles that resembled the sky-scapes. She knew they existed. Her grandparents used to go stone collecting, and find all sorts of stones that had been changed into miniature portraits and natural scenes, over the years, by the weather. Some looked like faces, like the sky, and some looked scenic.

Eileen turned away, set her face in a smile and approached the street leading to the cafe. Mrs. Lock wouldn't have remembered her, anyway.

She would re-introduce herself, and see if Mrs. Lock was now a Switch. If she wasn't Eileen would phone the purists and let them know where Mrs. Lock was.

Mrs Lock wouldn't have remembered Eileen even if she had a memory. Eileen was a non-descript sort of person who had planned her life to be non-descript. If she was ever caught committing a crime she wanted her victims or witnesses to scratch their heads thoughtfully, or at least wrinkle their eyebrow as they tried to describe her. If the actions were followed by a shrug she would feel that wearing her crowd scene clothes and hair had been worth it.

Mrs. Lock had lost her memory lots of times. It was as if a few brain cells had changed her memory's direction at the first shock she had, so the rest of her body could cope with whatever it was that was shocking her. That was just a small shock, and a small memory, but over the years the few cells had put up the equivalent of barricades, to divert the flow at each shock she had and at her every growing memories. When the barricades started to weaken and the memories started to seep back through she would feel like she had forgotten to do something small, like put on moisturiser, rather than remember what she had forgotten.

After the seep there would be a rush, a flooding, of memories, and she would feint again, before she remembered anything.

Her family called it 3d brain fever. She didn't know she had had 3d brain fever, because she had had 3d brain fever. 3d Brain fever caused amnesia. It was a catch-22 situation.

Some people had a warning of being sick by having an 'itch'.

The word 'witch' comes from 'itch'.

Her images weren't made from germs, or irritations, but they

146

might have been inspired by them. Being able to make lines and circles on the skin that communicated information was pretty cool. Mrs. Lock's images were prettier than a rash. Less 'uck' and more…interesting. If you wanted a busy health workers attention, you didn't want them to recoil at bubonic plague looking spots, you wanted them to come closer and prescribe antibiotics. A few words or pictograms on her skin describing her condition would definitely help her receive positive attention off a medic quicker than herpes-looking acne would. Medics were like that – they had a busy SMS life style that was hygienic and sterilised. They would appreciate her way of communicating. It was like she was texting them with her skin. She also had the advantage over the pus-ridden and flaky skinned as she didn't expel germs at anyone.

It was in her genetics that she was well mannered and less spitty. She was that way before she was born and it was like having a big nose or squidgy elbows. There was nothing she could do about it and nothing anybody else could do about it if they weren't born with the same gene - there was no point in anyone catching syphilis later in their life in the hope miniature picturesque lines will grow out of the bacteria, because it wasn't going to happen.

Mrs. Lock's skin was picturesque inside as well as out so her 3d brain fever was a bit of a nuisance for her. Her blood was a stream of shaped thoughts which took up lots of room. Words appeared on her tongue, in a slightly three dimensional way, and the whites of her eyes were occasionally diagrams made of blood vessels. Her eyes changed to green, blue and brown as her mind tried to be descriptive to what she was seeing.

The 3d brain fever mostly happened when too many thoughts happened at once. Her head swelled up, a little like a puffball, so the three dimensional thoughts had somewhere to store

147

themselves before they shrunk or dispersed. The brain, eyes, and ear-stuff took up all the regular available space so extra room had to be made.

If the ideas were creative then they could to be expressed, to make room. A quick watercolour would normally do, or perhaps a sculpture. Sometimes a quick mathematical problem would suffice. Mostly, reasonable logic shrunk most of her other thoughts to a manageable size, but if they stayed put they could give her a headache that could last up to a week. That was normal 3d brain fever but the amnesia made her forget she had a headache. Another strange side effect of her 3d amnesia was the more urgent the memory was to her immediate survival, the smaller it shrank, in the hope it could sneak through her nervous system undetected. Ironically, this meant that the more urgent it was, the less Mrs. Lock noticed it.

Unfortunately, and also in self defence, so she didn't give herself a shock, her eyes refused to see her skin, and she had given herself facial amnesia since she was born. She had tried to regain her memory, subconsciously, but despite using several types of water colours, re-reading old maths books and doing a bit of sculpturing to clear her mind, nothing had worked.

On the rare occasion she *did* catch a glimpse of herself the back log of thoughts and warnings her skin had wanted to show her all crowded for attention at the same time. (They were the only times her skin looked contagious.) She would have known how to deal with it, if only she could think. But if she thought, it would have caused a back log.

Rene was sitting silently, staring at the shop window.

The crowd seemed enormous.

She grabbed her laptop from her bag and held it, at arms length, in front of her.

148

Everyone was happy if the word 'laptop' was mentioned, or if one was seen.
People like to think the little machine had a use, just as the adverts had promised.

She had seen riots stop because of the appearance of a laptop in a crowd – it had that kind of calming influence and charm.

Laptops were never seen in riots, so there couldn't be a riot, was the kind of reasoning that had stopped them.

It was different if the laptop was being carried under the arm of a running window-breaker though. That was a signal to thieve.

Laptops with a swimming fish screen-saver was found to be the most effective at crowd stopping. They were associated with office work, or a compact, yet roomy, study space she supposed.
Mobile phones did not have the same effect. They were mostly associated with little buttons and cracked screens.
No one stared in at Rene, so she put the laptop back down and waited for Arthur to respond to the text she had just sent.

Graham looked around. A woman was in the middle of the path, slowly walking towards the top of the hill, her head held high.
He looked at her curiously. She didn't look as if she had prepared for this moment. She looked like a bag lady. Like Flow-chart. There was not a beauty pageant type dress hidden under the baggy coat. In her hand was a small hand bag while the other one held a supermarket plastic one. Her shoes were dark, and her jeans blue.
There wasn't any ceremonial dagger either, and she wasn't

covered in theatrical makeup.

All eyes were on her. Graham noticed that, though most were smiling at her fondly, a few were looking surprised, and a few were grimacing. The people smiling seemed to know who she was.

Most had their cameras directed at her.

He followed the lines of the cameras and suddenly spotted what they were looking at.

The woman's forehead, even at a distance, was obvious, if you knew to look there.

A face was appearing on her skin, slightly three dimensional. Everyone was looking at the mouth that was appearing, and a few were looking back at the sky above, as if comparing.

Graham looked at the sky, through the drizzle.

The clouds in front was identical to the one developing on the woman's face.

He looked back at the woman. She didn't look as if she was in pain. She looked as if she needed a tissue. Her eyes were looking round, nervously.

He watched with interest as a mouth appeared just above her eyebrows.

There were more smiles and groans when the lips had finished forming.

The mouth was not identical to Mrs. Locks own, but matched the cloud formation.

It was average sized, with no points or pouts. It wasn't thin or full lipped.

Mrs. Locks own mouth changed. It grew slightly bigger, and less stringy, looking more like the impression on her forehead and the one in the sky.

A slight, quiet applause started and finished as her mouth re made itself.

Mrs. Lock looked at her feet, then at the head in the sky. Her feet were the first thing she remembered. She had been bare footed, and there had been images of faces, ivy, roses, and a cup with a saucer balancing on the bridge of one of her feet. On the other there had been a fairy tale castle. It had scale skin as bricks. A princess, looking like herself, had been waving from a toe nail shaped window.

Mrs. Lock had been lying down, and she had feinted. When she had woken up, she had called her parents, and her face had reflected her mobile phone.

She had seen it in the mirror.

She didn't want to think about the rest; the days and nights which followed. It had all been too much. There had been visitors, and people at the door.

There had been cameras, like there was now.

The full face, on her forehead looked like a mask pulled up on to her temple.

Then everything harmlessly coincidental happened at once.

Mrs. Lock reached into her pocket for her mirror, as the mask-face seemingly slipped down over her own face. As she flipped the top off her mirror, the sky cloud face dispersed leaving a grey halo around part of the sun. It too looked like an open pocket mirror.

The crowd quietened at the simultaneous event.

She took another step forward and watched the cloud carefully. It was in this moment the fate of the weather would be shown.

The cloud, small and unimportant-looking, was on the brink of forming into a hurricane. That is what she was searching her mind for, not feinting farces, but the memories of just before she

151

was born.

If the hurricane was going to start then it would be here and now. The cloud itself was hundreds of miles away, but looked like it was only a hundred foot or so above.

Mrs. Lock held her breath, and took another step.

The crowd was searching her face, and looking at the matching cloud.

The Switches noted mirror matching mirror, and started to applaud. It was them, all them. Myra, facing Myra, across the sky, and across the earth. They were all and everything, and so was their reflection.

The grey dressed people filmed and watched for the next movements of air and skin. They were not as obvious in their surprise at the coincidence, but it showed. They would look at the film, again, later, when they were calmer, and see if Mrs. Lock had seen the mirror first. The sequence of events were important to them.

Eileen straightened her shoulders and opened the café door. The multitude had started to walk towards the cloud. She had half watched as she had rounded the corner. She had kept looking back, thinking she had seen a familiar face in the crowd, and the cloud had been in her eye line.

It was quite strange.

Arthur and Henry were recording it from the safety of the trees. They were sensible people.

Eileen was glad she had walked down to the café rather than wait for a look-a-like to turn up at the house. She would be trapped in her burrow, otherwise, if she had stayed inside. Burrow is a borrow. She didn't actually know who the house belonged to.

She let Henry deal with all that. Saying it was borrowed kept the house-head-hunters away.

Miranda was nowhere in the café.

Eileen raised her eyebrows at the café owner, who looked pointedly out of the window. She leaned against the door frame in tiredness. That was a worry. She had already left. Now she wouldn't be able to tell the difference if she saw another Miranda walking past. She gave the café a sweeping glance. A cult leader was sitting alone. At a table. It was Miss Runes. She was wearing The Necklace.

Eileen nearly feinted. A coven leader was sitting there, but there was no Mrs. Lock. 'Miss Runes?' she asked.

Violet looked up from her phone. 'Hello....' She replied and quickly typed in 'Miss Runes' on her phone. The woman's name was Eileen, and her face was Thursday night cult. She was Miranda's grandmother. What luck!

'......Eileen,' she added quickly. 'Do join me.' She looked at the information she had on her. She liked salads and had spots. That is why she had been told the name 'Miss Runes.' It was an obvious description of her own skin.

Mirror, mirror, I am no fool,
have your own name
to tell the cannibal.

'I am just texting. Won't be a moment. Would you like to share a salad?' she asked the woman.

Eileen was surprised that Miss.Runes had remembered her. She had only met her once or twice before. She was cult leader for her cult leader face. A woman that she must say hello to, no matter how distant from the Switches she had grown. She paid her pound a week to her own similar face, so no one would know she wasn't one of them anymore. In return she received a 'this-months' photo, signed with the cult leaders pseudonym. She had

had some odd names in the past- as if she had picked them up from a medical dictionary.

The faces had strict instruction not to call the cult leader by name if anyone else was about. They were only verbally allowed to address her if she was alone.

Eileen understood. Last month was a different name. Cult leaders had to change their name or they would be easier to stalk. Especially ones that looked like her.

'Miss Runes, what brings you here?' She asked, trying not to sound or seem nervous

The cult leader smiled. 'The weather.' She replied easily.

She stood up and shook Eileen's hand. 'Would you like to go and watch?'

Eileen nodded. Of course. It was the weather. She instantly felt livelier, and her spots shrunk to three, to indicate a cheer. Nothing to worry about. Not about Miranda at all.

Mrs. Lock was probably there to see the weather too.

Book of words;
Never shake hands if you suspect someone is a Switch.
Shaking hands, for those of you that don't know, is clasping someone else's hand in yours, and rising it up and down a few times, normally around the stomach or womb area.
For a Switch, who finds everything symbolic and meaningful - unless it is said in a comprehensive verbal language, plainly and clearly, then they can't understand a word, - shaking hands was a cannibalistic agreement. It meant that they would die by their own hand, which was their own twins. Or it meant from the womb to someone else's stomach, the hands being the link between both.

Also, try not to shake hands if you are an empathetic skin

154

talker. **Your body might try to change to have five extra fingers, as that part of the genetic coding that still builds may wonder why you are reaching for something that you already have. It wouldn't be a dramatic change – perhaps your hand might develop a little scratch, just so your genes can say they tried, but even that can get annoying over a period of time. You may start to wonder where and how you came to have a scratch, after totally forgetting it always happens after you shaked hands. Then you might start thinking it happened because of a lost needle, or a thorn catching on your clothes on the way home from somewhere and some bush.**
That sort of thinking may result in you sort of twirling around in circles occasionally, while checking the hem of the clothes you are wearing, which would make you look really thick.

Mrs. Lock looked slowly around.

She wondered if the people present knew.

There didn't seem to be one weather-watcher present. Well, not a serious temperature reading, wind monitoring fully qualified analyst there. And that is what she needed.

She took the next few steps in a rapid sprint, pulling out her phone as she did so.

The sugar packets spilt out of her pocket.

All the cameras followed the individual portions, as they scattered behind her. The photos would be analysed and mulled over, in a dark room.

She could see the cameras sweep backward and forwards, from behind her and then upwards, towards the sky.

When she looked up, the cloud pocket mirror was floating away.

Shafts of square sunlight sprung through the lilac clouds.

She rolled her eyes, at the coincidence, and connected to the

155

internet. The weather news only took a few seconds to load. She scrolled the page down, and looked for hurricane warnings.

☼

Graham looked at Mrs.Lock in disbelief. She *was* the bag lady, Flow chart, and amidst all the adoration and mysticism she was making a phone call. She had no sense of occasion, no suitable clothing and probably no credit. She had really spoilt the spiritual atmosphere that had developed. People who had previously been looking at her with open eyed amazement were now squinty eyed and confused.

They should have picked a better idol for the occasion, for whatever the occasion was for. He wondered if anyone would stop him if he moved closer, now she wasn't in pedestal position. Her forehead was giving him courage to look closer. He looked around nervously. Most eyes where on the sky, the rubbish she had dropped, and quite a few were still aimed at her face.

There were a couple of people at the top of the hill, holding out a box of some kind. He hadn't realised he had been walking to the top with her. It was subconscious. The whole crowd had been moving in a slow, intuitive, pre occupied way. The people holding the box were so close he could see their eye colour. They had been waiting, one with an arm outstretched, for over five minutes. He briefly turned his head to look at them. What a strong arm that woman had. He looked back at Mrs. Lock, who seemed oblivious. Her eyes had changed colour. They were grey.

Mrs. Lock put the phone away, with a disappointed look, before turning her attention back to the sky. There was no mention of anything unusual. It had reported sun, where there was rain, and then had stopped loading the web page. She tried to remember the warning signs.

She had known them before, so many years ago. Before she was

156

born and again afterwards. She had seen the common place but extraordinary sky and it had made sense to her, if only for a few minutes.

It was as if she had read the whole sky at once, as if it were a book; every formation of every cloud, and every space in between, that had floated past over the year had been enclosed within a few minutes of thought.

She couldn't remember rightly.

She looked ahead as the little hill top became slightly steeper.

A man and woman were standing a little way off. They looked like her parents. She couldn't tell the difference. They looked like so many people. The couple were holding out a box. The box was small and unimposing. She looked at them quizzically.

Perhaps they had seen her difficulty, and were offering her a mobile phone to use.

That would make more sense. Her parents wouldn't be standing on a wet and cloudy hill side, waiting for the coincidence of herself being there. She moved quickly, before they decided to put the presumed mobile phone in a dryer and safer place.

When she thought about it, they definitely couldn't be her parents. The people ahead of her were being slightly dramatic, and that wasn't like her parents either. Her parents were not stand-in-the-middle type of parents. They were more side-line parents. They looked like everyday shoppers, or commuters.

No one had ever really looked at them. They were non-colour, when in a crowd. These people looked uniformly smart and individual in their non-colour of grey, but would never look as non-colour as her parents.

She took another step. The couple smiled welcomingly, and made a giving gesture with the box.

Mrs. Lock reached out for it. To her disappointment it wasn't a mobile phone. It was a small coffin shaped casket. She looked at it curiously, and them wearily.

She had seen the jewellery casket before.

The woman reached across and tried to touch Mrs. Lock's cheek.

Chapter 8

The sky was becoming moodier. Not where they were focusing, but around the edges.

The path the people had made for Mrs. Lock had closed up behind her, except near the top of the hill.

It could be clearly seen by Eileen and the cult leader.

The cult leader smiled. It was for her. She could see some people at the top, waiting. She looked up at the sky. The cloud in the centre beamed with oblong freckled sunlight. The rainbow behind was spectacular, and the rain wasn't enough to damage her hairstyle.

She was used to crowds edging out of her way. She had never had to queue. Her height and beauty had always received the stand-back-and–admire reaction. She took advantage of the immediate stunning effect by stepping into the spaces that other people left. They had to stand back to see her face properly.

It was unusual to see a path at the top, and not at the bottom though. It was a large rectangle. Perhaps it was something to do with the shafts of light that had appeared in the clouds and her own imposing height. Her hair was also a long rectangle, which shone with blonde radiance. She mirrored the hilltop arrangement.

She took a step forward and the gap in front opened, just like it always had. She felt better now she had reverence. She took another step, and finding no resistance, started to stroll towards the top. Her identifying necklace sparkled like the rain in front of her, attracting attention from passing looks.

Eileen stood straight and followed. Her head was just behind the cult leader's armpit. She glorified in the interest she thought Miss Runes was attracting. Her skin burst out with two spots, then eight, followed by three. Looking at me, she told the world.

A slight breeze kicked up around their feet.

It wasn't aimed at just them. It was a general foot breeze that weaved and circled the whole crowd, but the cult leader, and Eileen, only saw their own hemlines being slightly rearranged.

They had reached the single portion sugar trail, which was still being photographed and avoided.

The sugar packets rose and danced with an unexpected gust, and with more coincidence, as they approached. The cult leader smiled enigmatically as the uplifting display renewed the crowd's interest.

She looked around, hoping that one of her coven had the scene captured in digital pixels. It wasn't the rubbish that she wanted to capture in a photograph, but the crowd all seemingly looking at her. The crowd itself, she had decided, wasn't worth her attention, but would look good in her photograph album. They were obviously rubbish-reading tramps. No one else would be that interested in the litter. She would edit the litter out.

Mrs. Lock, with the coffin shaped box in one hand, and with the other one fending off the over-familiar caress, froze.

The breeze circled around her legs. She turned and looked at the crowd.

She could see Miranda, just behind Graham, seemingly unaware of his presence. The wind had caught Miranda's hair, lifting it slightly. Miranda's hair was noticeable and chunky. Mrs. Lock looked at it curiously. The breeze was stronger than she thought.

She saw squinted eyes turn as one, to follow her own looks. Several people were staring at Miranda with the same interest.

Mrs. Lock shivered.

It was as if she was a baby again. Everything she had noticed, back then, became significant for everyone except herself. Then they would stare at her skin.

The coffin shaped box had been part of it all too. It had been there, along with the two faces that had been holding it. Her own parents looked the same age as the two in front of her.

They were doppelgangers, and spies of her baby life.

She tightened her grip on the coffin shaped box.

It was about two inches long.

Inside was an Emblem Seal, she was almost certain.

She felt her head swell with a rush of thoughts. They had opened the box and put the seal in her two day old hand. It had been the same size as her hand. It had looked like a small light house, but thinner, and more artistic. The top was a tiny sterling ball, covered in carved symbols. The body of it looked like plastic amber. The stripes were horizontal, in shades of brown, and of different band widths.

At the bottom was a white stripe. Underneath it made an octagon shape. In the centre was a tiny deer on a line of grass. The deer was an intaglio relief.

She had thought that the deer was an inverted face. The deer was made from pencil thin lines. From one angle it was a deer, prancing on a patch of land, but she could still see the inverted face in its lines as well. She could also see it as Glastonbury Tor too, as well as an eye.

But had they given it to her because of her skin? She was the inverted face. She was the mirror, facing the Myra.

161

She looked at the two people in front of her. The woman had looked disappointed when Mrs. Lock had raised her arm to brush her off, but now she was looking past her.

They both were.

Mrs. Lock turned her head to see what had captured their attention, slipping the coffin shaped box into her pocket as she did so.

A tall imposing woman was hundred yards away, moving in their direction. Mrs. Lock looked at her necklace enviously. It was a gem laden spectacle, which sparkled in the light rain. It took her a moment or two to realise she was in the wrong place, at the wrong time, with someone else's present in her pocket.

Her face reddened, and she stepped to one side. They, the two people who had gestured at her to take the little casket, had mistaken her for the woman's servant, probably. She shuffled backwards as they looked at the tall beautiful woman with admiration.

The grey suited people's eyes were still following her as she tried to hide in the crowd. Their faces had become the same scarlet tone as hers. They were embarrassed for her, probably. She had stolen a ceremonial gift.

She walked swiftly to a less uniform segment of the gathering and hid behind a fat man.

She took off her hat, put it in her bag, and pulled her hair out of a ponytail. She took off her coat and folded it over her arm. Her skin instantly aged. Her eyes turned a green colour and her height grew and thinned.

She walked away, towards a grassy embankment. She would sit behind it and think what to do next.

The breeze had hung onto her coat for a few seconds, holding it horizontal and shielding her movements from the eyes of the greys.

The seal may have been to test her baby health, she had first thought. The woman had nodded at her, and she had closed her fingers around the stem of it. They wanted to see if she could grip it, she supposed. She had tried to hold on to it.

Why they wanted to give the emblem to the tall woman behind her, she didn't know.

She sat behind the mound. Her headache was threatening her not to try to remember any more.

She was out of sight from most of the crowd. She thought she could see Miranda, at the edge of them, looking towards her, but she thought she could also see the grey clothed people staring at her too. Her imagined self-importance had tricked her eyes, she hoped. Adrenaline was making her eyes stupid.

She reached into her pocket and pulled out the coffin box. She just wanted to see if what she remembered was true, then she would return the box.

She would make a cushion, by folding her coat, and making it look ceremonial for when she gave it back. It was velvet green so would suit the object. The casket could lay in the middle.

She would present it back to them with a stylish setting, and they would think that is why she had walked away with it.

She reddened again, not just with the stupid idea, but because, just for a few minutes she had imagined that they had been waiting for her.

It was her skin's ego, not hers.

Another twinge crowded her head.

She closed her eyes while she waited for the ache to recede.

The small casket was like an old fashioned ring box, but longer. It was a dark speckled blue with a gold trim around the edge, and made of paper mache. A small brass clasp held it shut.

She held it under her coat, away from the rain, and opened it.

Inside was what she imagined to be there. It was smaller than she remembered, but was identical to the one of her first days.

She held on to the small hoop at the top of it, and lifted it out of its case.

When held up to the rainy sunlight, the bands of amber coloured plastic glowed and changed colour.

She moved it to one side, in order to see it better, noticing as she did so the shafts of light that were still forming out of the clouds. They were all rectangular and the pattern in which they were appearing matched the lighter sections of the emblem seal, exactly.

She looked at the seal closer. It seemed that if she held it up to the sky, the darker bands would match the clouds.

The sky was crowded with similar looking patterns of light and dark.

Mrs. Lock squinted her eyes. Holding the emblem seal up, she tried to line it up with the shafts of sunlight that were still appearing in the cloud above. She tried several different directions, before she found the patch of cloud and the light that fitted the emblem seal pattern exactly.

There were no dramatic laser-like shafts of light when she found the matching part, like she hoped there would be, so there was nothing to warn her of what happened next.

The light looked as if it was shining through the lighter segments of the emblem seal.

Then, in unexpected energy, it seemed to be in her face with an invisible force.

She passed out.

There was no real outward change to the scene. Miranda saw Mrs. Lock take something from her pocket, hold it up to the light, and then drop it. It looked to Miranda as if it was a twisted sugar packet.
Miranda walked faster. Mrs. Lock had seemed to have feinted. The sugar packet had been dropped, and she had slid down the little mound she had been leaning on. Her head leaned to one side, and her grey hair glittered in the sun.

Graham half turned as Miranda pushed by him.
He had thought it was her in front of him, but was never fooled by hairstyles, so hadn't called out to her.
He had seen several Miranda hairstyles since he had joined the crowded hill top; there was an unusually large amount, for this area.
He had felt the urge to communicate with them all but had restrained himself from jumping up and down and waving.

It wasn't that sort of crowd anyway.

It was a more quiet and dignified type of gathering. They all looked as if they had turned up for a business meeting.
This Miranda hadn't looked at him, but past him, to where Flow Chart had walked.
He had watched Flow Chart with interest, and then with embarrassment for her, as the real star of their gathering appeared.
He could tell who the gathering was for, at once, since the coven leader had come into view. She was tall, imposing and beautiful.

165

She looked ready and dressed for crowd pleasing. She had the dignity and style for being the centre of attention.

Graham had watched silently, with admiration, as she had timed her walk to coincide with the breezes. The sugar packets had lifted with precise and seemingly coordinated flutterings.

The sugar packets had held his gaze, for a second or two. Sugar portions were not that light. They were not weighty, but it took more than a soft wind to lift them.

He would have thought more about weight and force ratio if the woman had been as dull looking as Mrs. Lock, but, as he had already noted, she *was* beautiful.

He had gazed at her as her eyes swept the crowd. He could have fallen in love with her, if she had singled him out. She was amazing.

But a Miranda had pushed past him, as if she had been watching him all along. He thought he recognised her perfume, and the way one chunky curl bounced on her shoulder, out of place with the rest of her hair.

He reluctantly followed her, with a subconscious sureness that it was her.

The whole crowd were moving in the same direction anyway.

Eileen and the cult leader looked as the gathering moved passed them.

There were apologetic looks in the cult leader's direction, and a few 'call you' hand movements.

The 'call you' hand movements consisted of an empty, gripping hand being put towards the cheek a couple of times, as if the person was hitting themselves, or grabbing at their own jowl, and a lifting of the chin.

It was strange, but typical Switches thought that aggravating someone to the point of them threatening violence would make them look popular because of that 'call you' hand to face movement. Some of them extended this weird thought to actual violence, and started to hit people on their arms in an aggressive, chummy type of way, in the hope it would produce a phone call action, in their direction. 'Hit', they said, was so similar to the word 'hint' that one day someone would make the connection.

The cult leader was sure that, for her, it was always 'call you'.

In her earlier days it may have been a threat of violence, but she used to dress as a boy and do a bit of intimidating, back then, so that hadn't surprised her.
She half closed her eyes, guarding them in memory of her teenage lifestyle.
She looked as if she was flirting with the crowd. A few more men made the 'call you' gesture, before moving on.

The crowds continuing right angled moving behaviour was a bit confusing.
The cult leader looked over them.
She was wondering whether there was something looming over the prow of the hill, which had made them change direction. The clouds above the hill were looking a tiny bit more imposing than they had been. They *were* beginning to loom.
There was not enough looming for the crowd to do a complete square, or a 'u', turn though.
She watched the heads bob pass with a disappointed glare. The welcoming couple at the top of the hill had also made a sideways turn.
She looked at Eileen, who spontaneously acned at her. Too much sugar, the cult leader thought, was bad for the skin. She looked back at the dancing packets, which had now become too wet to lift. They were still being photographed by passing cameras as

they rested in their new arrangement.

She turned further around and stared at the packets. They looked different from this angle. The passing mob hadn't seemed to have noticed, probably because of the direction they were looking at them from. Curiously, she retraced her footsteps, back to the wind blown sugar. The individual sugar packets looked as if they were a couple of letters, with a profile of a face.

The letters seemed to be in some old font; twirly and three dimensional. Shadows made up some of the letters. She squinted her eyes. The letters seemed to be 'G. Z '. They were quite clear, from where she was standing. The profile of the face was just as lucid. The face looked as if it was grimacing.

The cult leader pulled out her mobile phone, and started to photograph the site, before the rain washed it away. If she could get to the other side of it, she could see if it looked any different from another angle too.

She side stepped her way through the crowd, ignoring them as she clicked her camera.

The crowd huddled around Mrs. Lock.

The emblem seal had been hurriedly picked up by the couple who had presented it to her, and placed back in its box. The box had been shoved in Mrs. Lock's bag, which was still clasped in one hand.

Her face had been swollen with lines and images.

The harder, deeper lines matched the emblem's stripes of light. Finer lines crowded the parts inside the divisions.

The skin that had been in front of the darker, amber bands of the emblem was overlapping with images, numbers and letters, and was slightly less swollen. Her face was varying shades of black, reds, yellows and white. She did not look burned, but as if the rainbow behind the clouds had given her the colours.

She looked very ill, and very similar to a woodchip notice board.

168

Her arms were flung out. One hand was still holding her bag, the other was relaxed, but at shoulder height, as if she was trying to fly with one arm. That hand was in the shadow, made by a nearby man.

It was image and scar free. The casket presenter nodded towards her hand, as he tucked the casket in Mrs. Lock's bag.

The crowd looked at each other. One near the back shrugged and another scratched his ear.

A few others moved closer, so Mrs. Locks face was in their shadows.

There was a dramatic pause in movement as they waited for something to de-happen.

Most of them were used to Mrs. Lock's reaction to the sun, so her theatrical face was nothing new to them.

They had sat, or stood quite near, over the years, as Mrs. Lock had feinted, grown old, grown young, became devil like, had picture-gramed whole essays at them, and animated cartoons within distance. They had a book case full of photos of her face, and boxes of videos that showed her extraordinary skin and its different qualities.

The looks on her face, as she lay there, were rare for her normal differences, but not fatal, they hoped. They entwined her looks with the weather, and fatal for her may mean fatal for the country. They told the weather by her skin. She was their barometer. She was their Sky news. She couldn't die.

Cameras were clicking and videos being made and uploaded as her skin edged its way to normality.

The crowd gave an expected nod as the swelling started to instantly recede. They also gave a little gasp. The collective gasp was for newcomers and the video players, really. They were not that impressed by Mrs. Lock's morphing skin. They had been, but now the amazement had become sustained interest. They were politely shuffling for the best position for filming, while trying to maintain a newness about them, as the less grey people looked with genuine shock.

The greys didn't think they were being cruel by their watching only stance. They had never known how to relieve Mrs. Lock's discomfiture, if she was feeling any, except by shielding her from the sun. They couldn't ask her if she was in pain, because then she would notice that they had been watching her. That would scare her, and they didn't want to scare her, so they generally did a lot of slight manoeuvring around her instead. They sort of felt she looked at them the same way she regarded trees or pieces of landscaping. She didn't really notice them and wouldn't notice them unless someone told her to. With the scenery, it would be a tourist friendly sign pointing out that it was a constant feature of the landscape. With them it would be them verbalising themselves by saying they were there. If they did that, then she would suddenly realise, and then feint even harder than she normally did.

It was a difficult moral decision for them, but as the years had passed, it had become habitual for them to mostly watch and shuffle. If asked, one or two may have said that asking Mrs. Lock about her health would have been like finally asking their partners name after years of ignorance. They hadn't asked in the beginning, so they couldn't ask now.

Other, new, onlookers may not feel the same nonchalance about their lack of direct interest in her health, so they had to pretend to be the same new.

One silently mouthed 'wow', for effect.

A few more greys shuffled even closer.

Mrs. Lock was face to feet with rain splattered, shiny polished shoes that edged her whole body.

Her face was still striped, and her eyes still closed, but the swelling lessened even further in the shadows of the people who were surrounding her.

From a distance Mrs. Lock could not be seen. The group still looked like a group, and not like an impromptu first-aid committee. Most of the cameras appeared as if they were still aimed at the sky, which had become filled with images similar to the ones on Mrs. Locks face. The images were over spilled and confused, when left in the clouds. They mixed themselves into bulbous features and top heavy arrangements. On Mrs. Locks face they gained a realistic ratio. 'U''s became like half an eye shapes, or like bottom lips. The clouds that had looked like bent tree trunks become short, little necks on her skin.

If it had been sunset, the sky would have looked like a painting of an overcrowded hell, but in the daylight, with the hazy pale blue sky behind, the busy clouds looked more like an exaggerated caricature of the crowd beneath.

Miranda reached Mrs. Lock the same time the crowd had, but she had been manoeuvred away from her.

She had been left standing behind a particularly red ear, and a bristly jaw.

She was new to Mrs.Lock-watching. A few had noticed her newness, and had surreptitiously taken photographs. The people there were good at sneaky photography. They noted everyone, and everything. It was for safety. They didn't want to be followed home.

Miranda had been standing near to Mrs. Lock, looking at her with a shocked expression. The people surrounding her, even though they were protecting her with their varying postures, were there to film her.

When she bent down, to ground level and tugged Mrs. Locks elbow, there had been more flashes of minuscule movement on the edge of her peripheral, as they slightly turned their mobile phones.

Ignoring them, she had tugged at the elbow again, 'Mrs. Lock?'
she asked.

The crowd exchanged looks.

This never happened. No one ever directly approached Mrs.
Lock. In thirty years of Lock watching, this was a first.

One of the greys squinted his eyes at Miranda, as if she was
behaving suspiciously.

'Shall we get her undercover, perhaps the café? Or the cinema?
That might be nearer.'

The crowd looked at their feet and at each other.

No one said anything, then, as one, and just as Graham said 'I'll
help', the nearest grey clothed people simultaneously bent their
knees, in a ready-to-pick-up-position.

Mrs. Lock did not notice being lifted up and steadily carried. Her
head was still protected from the heat, by stray coat hems and
bent waists. It had taken a few more people than they had
thought it would to lift her; she was heavier than she looked. She
seemed even fatter, when she was unconscious.

Her head was supported by Miranda, who had been shuffled
around to a position that suited her height.

Graham was walking just behind her, and Miranda had
acknowledged his presence, with a distracted smile. She was still
intrigued by Mrs. Lock's skin. Mrs. Lock seemed to know she
was there. Her chin skin had slightly morphed, to imitate eyes,
one on either side of it, looking at Miranda. It was a good sign.
Mrs. Lock wasn't dead. She was narcissus, looking up her nose,
like it was a love heart in between her image eyes and her real
eyes. The looks of the chin eyes were unnerving, but Miranda
could not look away from her skin. Other parts of her face were
alive with images too. There was a goat on Mrs. Lock's cheek,
and a shopping coupon floating on her forehead. Miranda smiled.
Mrs. Lock was dreaming and still cloudy. The stripes across her
face now looked like spaced rain. The impression was so strong
that the images of the rain drops were leaving pitted marks on

Mrs. Lock's skin.

Miranda looked up. It was raining less now, but the wind was a little stronger. She couldn't feel it much, surrounded by people, but the trees were making a seashore noise. The clouds above were a shade darker, matching the colours of the horizon almost completely. Miranda wasn't normally a cloud watcher, so she was impressed by the scenic views the clouds were making, and particularly intrigued by the similarity they had to Mrs. Locks face.

Above was a loose egg timer shape, formed from the clouds, and sitting near the centre of Miranda's vision. It was thin and long looking. It was Mrs. Locks face again. The two ends of the egg timer looked like eyes. Mrs. Lock had mirrored it,.

If Mrs. Lock had been awake she would have waved her arms about, perhaps, and cried out 'Innocent-looking typhoon! Innocent looking typhoon!' and the crowd would have moved a bit faster, but she was still feint and silent. One of her wrists did a quick graphic chart, concerning wind speeds, and altitude, to warn them, but it was totally ignored, as it was hidden by a swishing hip length jacket lining.

Chapter 9

Her Graham watched Graham with fascination, a red face, and with Graham's mother offering him a tissue. She had had one of those moments when she recognised something wasn't normal about Graham, and thought if he covered his face, she would feel a little bit better about looking at him.

A tissue, from her point of view, would suffice. She was shorter than him, so was unable to avoid his nose.

Graham was a twin for this pair of nostrils. If the nostrils were covered she might be able to see his other characteristics more clearly.

The nose was blinding her to 'her Grahams' less similar facial bits.

She hadn't thought this consciously. Consciously she thought that he was Graham.

She was holding the tissue at shoulder height, in readiness for a son's easy acceptance, and was looking around her at the same time. As she was shorter she could not see through the crowd, as Her Graham could.

She was excited. If she had known that most of the people gathering would be men of acceptable good looks, she would have made more of an effort with her appearance. It isn't nice to embarrass nice looking men with a crumpled coat and badly dyed hair. It didn't look good in family photographs, and cost a lot of time with photo editing and stuff like that. She didn't think she looked too bad. She would be alright as long as she didn't take her coat off. She was wearing frayed shorts and a t-shirt with 'Remember 287' written on it. It would be too bad if it was one of those pay-again switch-alls, or, as it was pronounced now, a 'pagan ritual'. They dropped the 'Y' and 'I' out of the spelling, so everyone would know they objected for paying again, when their twin had already paid.

Graham's mother didn't like those sort of people. They were the people that made her behave weird, by kitchen windows.

She would make menstrual cycle excuses, if that is what the gathering was about.

The grey people looked decent, even though they were taking her photo, thinking that she hadn't noticed. They had clean collars and neat haircuts. Some showed they were men by having a slightly unshaven look, which she appreciated.

Bare faced men could be women, or, even worse, men who thought that they looked baby-like. She couldn't relate to baby-like. They were nearly almost always Switches, in her experience. She was from a small village though, so she must make allowances for big city fashion. That is where these people looked like they were from. The some of the smooth faces she did spot were masculine in other ways. She could tell they were men.

Then there were the other people. They weren't local either. They weren't the same as the grey clothed people. They were dressed like people who had taken a detour from shopping, and had ended up in a field.

No one was looking at her. For a moment she had felt film star like, while the cameras had been aimed her way, but that feeling had been instantly replaced with one of shame. It wasn't as if she had done anything wrong, but her mind instantly linked cameras straight to CTV surveillance, so it jumped straight to false admittance as she didn't want any interrogation bits in the middle.

Still holding the tissue out, she turned her head to look at her house, instantly regretting it as she did. Now she would be on her own CTV tape, behaving in an annoying manner, and not as she would like to be seen.

She would probably be copied, as well, by a look-a-like, holding a tissue out, while bending her head backwards. They were like that.

She knew that this time next summer, there would be someone standing in exactly the same place, standing in the exact same pose, and she would know for definite that she was being stalked. She shivered and turned back, wondering which member of the crowd would blow up the photo, and sell it on. They were all looking at the sky though, and moving forward, at a slow pace, towards the village. It was now a procession. She didn't like processions. They were normally morbid events that marked deaths or memorials. She looked up at Graham, who was looking at her in a glazed eyed way. He hadn't taken the tissue, and she felt stupid.

'C'mon.' She said, and started to follow the crowd.

The sky, she noticed, wasn't the same as it usually was over this way. It must be the visiting people that had made it different. There was a lot of body heat mingling in the air and the village was at a high attitude. This morning's low cloud had probably been disturbed and mixed with city dwellers sweat. They went to work on an egg, apparently, and that cloud looked like a very thin, very long egg-timer. The idea she was watching the crowds thoughts, above her, instantly transformed her mood of foreboding into one of interest.

She concentrated on them as she walked, forgetting about Her Graham, who was now trailing behind her.

Her Graham had been looking at the tissue with equal awareness. He didn't know what she was trying to show him, but the tissue had looked very similar to an origami swan, or perhaps a drake duck. Why she showed her son random pieces of origami, he didn't know, but he had showed an un-son-like lack-of-attention to it, he thought. He had looked at the tissue with more of a distant audience gaze, so had hinted he wasn't the person she thought he was.

It hadn't worked.

He followed, promising himself he would be more obvious the next time he communicated with her.

From the book of words; No one knew who made the clouds their amusing and interesting shapes, but most had presumed it was to do with radio waves, of different frequencies. The sky was where old text messages went to die, or, sadly, where unanswered voice messages waited to be collected by the already dead. The voice messages were in the form of pictograms and the text messages were numbers and letters. The clouds were a virtual graveyard and *was* the space trash that politicians argued about.

Graham looked at Mrs. Locks face, then nervously at Miranda. He was trying to catch her eye. The woman looked radio active to him, now he had thought about it. She had cloudscapes all over her neck wrists, and face. She was contaminated by missing icons and rejected SMS. He moved back a step. She was unconscious and radiating at him. She might explode at any moment.

He thought of the sugar packets, and how they had danced when she dropped them. She had given them radio sickness. They were eaten-the-credit, looking-for-the-sugar-lump-game-app sugar packets now, after they had been near her. He could tell. If he put one of those in his soya-milk coffee, it would be pulling faces and asking if he had any vanilla flavouring to add.

He squinted his eyes. The sugar packets had already started to communicate. They had spelt out letters. To him it had looked as if the letters had spelt out 'Gzk'

'Gzk' were initials that meant radio-wave, plus speed, plus weight. He had learnt that from an old physics book, which was kept in the attic, waiting for a time of intellectual revival. 'Gz' was short for gigahertz, and the 'k' was the static energy that the radio waves created; it was the weight of the polarised atom.

Why the letters had formed on the path, he had no idea. He looked at 'Flow Chart'. She was very fizzy looking. All her skin was moving, while staying in the same place. She was completely 'tuned in', as the old hippies used to say. She was unconscious still.

He looked at Miranda again, to see whether she was affected. Something had jumped from the sky, and had landed on Mrs. Lock as she had walked up the hill, he was sure of it. Some kind of radio atomic sub-particle gun had knobbled her as she had tried to join the throng.

Miranda's face was free of mobile phone awareness.

He looked slowly around at the grey clothed people. They began to look ominous. They looked like retired radiologists and over qualified astronomers, rather than day tripping commuters, which is what he had first thought they were. He slowly slid his eyes down to pocket level, suddenly aware of weaponry and death bringing gadgets.

He had a quick realisation why the word 'gay' had become popular for homosexuals – '**ray**' gun and 'gay' are two similar when it is just eye-talk - and turned his head away.

He wasn't the only man to wonder about these grey people, and think about what they kept in their trouser pockets. He might be the only one that thought 'Gzk ray –gun' rather than 'mobile phone' though. He couldn't see anything, but nothing was about

179

the size of what he was looking for. It was useless, really. Technology was too camouflaged for the human eye. For him.

He looked up to the sky, and wondered why he hadn't just stayed in and took photos from there instead. It would have been a lot simpler and he wouldn't have looked like he was trying to pick men up. He would have had some great photos to study. He could hardly see anything from where he was standing, but, he supposed, he did have the advantage of studying Flow Chart close up.

He would probably never see Gzk in action again.

He looked at her face, keeping his hands away from anyone that was actually touching her. It was fascinating.

The crowd had reached the High Street. They hadn't expected this to happen. Mrs. Lock normally feinted, but it was always in a convenient spot. There was always something soft for her to lounge back on, and she always feinted within toilet distance. It was something some of the grey crowd had noted. They had actually measured the distance, disguised as workmen. It was something that interested them, and they had made graphs and pie charts with the collected data. The nearest toilet always varied between twenty to fifty feet. They didn't count the distances she had feinted in her own living area.

Their calculations looked more like IP addresses, when written down. Twenty-one feet, thirty-seven inches, nought point forty-five of an inch was spelt 210.037.450.001. They had fun imagining where Mrs. Lock thought she was, while sleeping, as more images normally appeared on her skin while she snored.

They frequently tried to find the IP addresses that the measurements looked like, because they got very bored and read a lot of comic science fiction.

They also played with the numbers by converting them in to

phone numbers, and by changing them into corresponding letters, they could play anagrams with them. It helped make sense, they said, of her physiology. Also they had already completed all the brain-teaser books, so had to make up their own fun.

A few of the grey people had stayed behind to inspect the mound she had feinted on, and had taken photos and samples of the grass there. One had a measuring glint in his eye. This was the longest distance, from the toilet, that Mrs. Lock had ever given them to play with.

Some of the men carrying Mrs. Lock had started to sweat, half way down. She was a heavy woman, but particularly heavy when carried only with one hand. Those that didn't start sweating were wondered at for there immensely strong finger digits. Mrs. Lock hadn't been raised above them, as they had wanted to watch her face, so, with a small amount of choreography, they had placed themselves in a single file of one-handed carriers, with feet moving in a slow march.
Now they were at the High Street they gently lowered themselves to place Mrs. Lock on a convenient piece of grass. One idly looked around for the usual toilet and a few others massaged the blood back in to their fingers.

Graham looked at Miranda. 'Hello.' He said.
Miranda looked at him. 'Graham?'
Graham smiled. 'Cirrus?'
Miranda shook her head. 'No, I don't think that is what that one is. Look closer.' But she squeezed his hand and smiled, as she leaned forwards to peer at Mrs. Locks face. 'It looks more like a rabbit, with a carrot.'
Graham edged his head backwards while still peering at Mrs. Lock from the corner of his retreating eyes. Laying down she looked like a particularly yeasty pancake. Her head reminded

him of an allotment potato. The one that no-one wanted to peel, because of its unusual traits and knobbly bits.

He wanted the other woman to be there instead. She was less offensive to the eyes.

Miranda moved forward, into kissing position, but really, he couldn't. She might have been potatoed by the tramp, Flow Chart woman, without being aware of it.

Mrs Lock woke up. 'Ahh, I wondered where you'd gone. There's one more bourbon left,' Mrs. Locks hand was hovering in front of her, as if there was a plate there, but then she scowled, '*if you want it.*' She said at Miranda, before closing her eyes again.

The crowd, still filming, smiled at each other, as if she was a pleasing child. She was lucid, and food thinking. Perhaps, Miranda thought, that they had better take her back to the café. The café was nearer, and the smell of food might wake her. She leant over Mrs. Lock. 'Would you like some sugar-free, gluten free, wheat free chocolate biscuits now instead? 'She shouted. There was no instant reaction but when she added, 'I 'll pay,' in a louder voice, Mrs. Lock's skin looked at her. Rather, the skin on either side of her chin gently changed a shade, so it looked as if she was showing an interest in Miranda.

Miranda squinted her eyes, and looked at the sky. She was slowly learning what was Mrs. Lock, and what was clouds on her face. On first glance, the clouds hadn't changed, but it was getting windier. It was stronger every gust.

Mrs. Lock was the only person who seemed to be fat enough to survive if it became even gustier. She was built for bad weather. Everyone knew that the wind didn't pick up pebbles and leafs. Mrs. Lock was built like both. She was a pebble lying on a leaf, with that stomach.

Mrs. Lock was safe if Miranda had to suddenly run for cover, in to the nearest shop, the church, or the nearby bus stop. She would probably just turn over and reach for another invisible, non-existent comestible.

Miranda looked around for someone to help her carry Mrs. Lock to the café. The crowd had mostly spilled into the small village High Street, and were still eagerly pointing cameras in their direction. She pointed in the direction of the nearby café, in response to questioning looks, and bent down again to support Mrs. Locks head.

Arthur and Henry had slowly slid away from the covering of the trees and had been slowly walking towards the village. Arthur was walking a little faster, in the hope that Rene was still safe. Henry was filming and muttering. His leg, he said, had definitely been cursed. Therefore, he explained, that nice woman who he had met on holiday, for several years, back in the nineteen nineties, hadn't been talking to him for polite reasons, but had been trying to get him to drop his wallet. He thought she had been a bit weird. Young women didn't chat that intimately to unknown old men. She had been positively flirty. Her eyes had flickered this way and that every time they had had an encounter at the vegan pastry counter. 'Arthur, have a look at my chest, will you, to see if what I think is true?'

Henry's subconscious said a lot about what he accurately knew, when his actual person thought otherwise. It was mostly vanity and hope that made him ignore any directive that come at him from himself.

Henry was limping, and Arthur hoped it *was* a psychological curse. He didn't know what to do about physical limps. Physical limps were inverted physical lumps, he supposed. When something was poked in, it probably poked out somewhere else. It was the law of displacement. Curing them was a matter of intense observation probably, and a good knowledge of origami,

183

but only the origami that was the folded paper game. The paper folded game could open to reveal answers to questions. The top had numbers on it that represented a lump or a limp on a limb. If a pin was pushed in to the folded paper, through one of the numbers on the top when paper was unfolded, the pin inserts showed a prediction of innys and outey displacements. The inside was usually painted with the figure of a body.

Arthur supposed curing someone depended on if you, or the patient, thought the zygote was a folded paper square or not.

Arthur had stopped fumbling with his feet and hands but was worried to see that the feared crowds had reappeared in the High Street. They had all gone but were now back. They were obviously focusing on the sky, not on invisible buildings. They were also showing an interest in a section of badly laid pavement and a grassy clearing. He was quite curious at to why a small group had divided into two close lines and had started shuffling towards the café. His throat had constricted in a worried way. What they were carrying was just out of sight, but Miranda, or someone like her, was looking down at something. She was at the back of the group. They looked like a shuffling horizontal brick archway.

He turned to look at Henry, who was exposing his chest to him. He presented his upper body with a couple of emphasizing jerks, as if he was a topless model that no one was noticing, and was looking down at it himself with a searching gaze.

'Yes, Henry. I can see who you mean. She was particularly interested in your debit card. I agree with your chest. She did curse you, I think, but please put your hairy nipples away, and look down there. Is that Miranda and Graham?'

Henry took a few steps forward. His chest showed Miranda and the gang she was with. Arthur half turned his head away from the sight. They looked like a vagina, from Henry's subconscious point of view.

He had his hands around his armpits, already pulling his top

184

down as he walked towards Arthur.

'See.' He said, 'She has got worse.'

Arthur paled. He wondered who, or what they were carrying. He quickened his step, but his hands and feet fumbled more than they had before. His nervous reaction had grown to fit his imaginings.

It was sad. The flowing movement of the grey people had started to lull him into a slight tremble rather than a full shaking of the limbs, but now they looked like a savage jungle scene. The bizarre weather didn't help. The wind was coming at them in gusts, but the rain danced with it by not falling when the gusts occurred. The rain jumped into the spaces the wind left, falling horizontally between each burst. The rainbow and sun was still lightning the rain with a speckled sparkly effect. It was like being in a film scene, Arthur decided, which calmed him down a little bit more. He could act. Pretending to be someone else helped him forget his own personality. His face was always cast as a hero. It made him feel heroic. It made him behave heroically.

'C'mon' he said to Henry, and quickened his step.

The café was cramped. The greys had pushed a few tables together and had slowly lifted Mrs. Lock on to them. She was breathing regularly, and her skin was slowly healing as she was out of the sunlight. One thoughtful man, a less grey one, had placed a chair over her head, to block out the other light sources.

She had been squared, and shadowed. It was a bizarre sight. Her handbag and shopping bag had been placed on the chair above and a few skin image fans were sitting as near to the exposed flesh as they could get. Their eyes and cameras were a few centimetres away from her head, hands and ankles.

Eileen and Miss Runes stood by the café window, peering in.

185

Miss. Runes knew that the horrible old woman had feinted on purpose. Some people were like that. Grabbing the pity from the hand, she called it, by grabbing attention like that. They couldn't wait for the hand to be offered naturally. The lines in the palm of the hand spelt 'pity'. She knows. She had spent years rubbing hers with hand cream, looking at every wrinkle and dent, while trying to get rid of them. It was a hard lined font of an alphabet, they spelt, and the woman on the table was a hard lined old crone.

She studied her reflection in the window. It wasn't surprising that other women needed to take drastic action to get a man's attention, with her presence. With her beauty, no man would look at another woman without it.

Eileen peered through the glass. It was a bizarre sight. Mrs. Lock was lolling on some table, with a chair over her head. It was like some arty, modernistic version of a devil worshipping group. She expects someone had asked 'when is a pentagram not a pentagram?' and the answer had been 'when it is a chair.' Or perhaps Mrs. Locks face had an image of the pentagram that they usually drew on the floor, so they had tried to fit a chair in the middle of it by putting it above.

Eileen's eyes drifted to an unseen area as she imagined pizzas with the little plastic white stands, which used to be placed in the middle of them to stop the pizza from sticking to the cardboard box.

That was the size they needed, not that great big thing.

Eileen remembered one of her coven having photos of Mrs. Locks face, disguised as night time. She did actually have stars and a quarter moon doodle, but they weren't realistic enough to have their own devil worshipping group. A devil worshipping group wouldn't fit on her cheek anyway.

That lot in the café might be have been persuaded that having a full size chair would do, but she wasn't convinced.

She moved her head closer to the window, to see it better. The coven usually put the chair in the centre of the pentagram and their victim on top. It was to do with the quarter moon, bottoms and a pentagram. It was all very anal, and retentive, and all to do with the shape of the anus, being a star shape. The victim was the celebrity 'star' that was the anal 'star' that was seat. That meant they were 'eat'.

Eileen looked curiously at the chair seat, by standing on tip toe and leaning closer to the shop front.

It looked as if they had already eaten what was on the chair, and left the skin there, in the shape of bags.

They were *very* arty, she thought and *very* forward-looking. A person hadn't been in the chair, nor had an animal been eaten, skinned and made into bags, but perhaps they were admitting to eating a couple of veggie burgers. The bags looked like empty wrappers, and one had recyclable' written on it.

Made a change for them, she supposed, and saved them a lot of bother.

Her view was suddenly blocked by a reflecting face, who nodded at her before taking a photo.

Eileen jumped back, as far as she could. Outside of the café was crowded with people, huddling from the rain. Half had their backs to her, staring at the sky, and about half were staring at the window, trying to catch a glimpse of Mrs. Lock. She stepped on to someone's foot, and elbowed another in his back, in her surprise. Unknowingly, her face had spotted itself with five pimples. She had thought pentagram, and the man at the window had thought she had exposed 'Is she alive?'

Eileen was still full of curiosity as to why Mrs. Lock was on the table. They could have just taken her to the community hall, or the church.

She looked at Miss Runes, who was pouting at her reflection, and blowing kisses at herself. She would be able to get them into the café, through the throng of people, if she wanted to. She manoeuvred herself into an angle that Miss. Runes could see, and made eye movements towards the café door.

Miss. Runes nodded. They were such easy challenges for her to win.

Forgetting her present demure, she bent down, ready to lift the people obstacles out of her way, before remembering that she wasn't a thug teenager anymore. She looked at the nearest man, not even bothering to change her face into a more welcoming look, and he instantly moved for her, with a smile forming on his lips.

She reached the door in a few steps and gestured for Eileen to join her, before looking slowly around the fat woman with the ego problem. The tables had been moved to accommodate her fatness. One little move, and she would slip in between the tables as they parted. Miss. Runes smirked as she stashed the thought for when it was needed. The rest of the café was full of people. She looked at the table she had been sitting at. It still hadn't been cleaned and the table was conspicuous by being the only table that was littered.

The glimpse turned into a stare. She pulled out her mobile and flicked through her photos.

The rubbish was arranged in the same pattern that had been left on the path that had been made out of sugar packets. The table edges looked as if it was the path border. She took a photo.

Eileen hadn't notice Miranda yet. She had. Now she wanted to talk to her. She wanted to know what it meant.

Crowds heave, mobs energise, audiences dance and rioters stomp. Arthur memorised the differences as he approached the High Street and the varying appearances.

And commuters looked innocent and looked at the sky. He liked to think the grey clothed people were commuters. They hardly ever got to see the sky staying in the same place, so it would be natural for them to be stunned into staring. They only got to see it from the train or a car window normally. It was unhealthy really. He knew. Nineteen thirty trains had pull down shades so the travellers didn't let the sky think for them.

Image clouds had that effect on people. Seen from a train, they were faster images, that some imagined could easily replace the natural thoughts of a casual observer. Clouds that drifted away were a lot easier on the mind than train clouds. The train clouds trained the commuters into regular odd habits.

Commuters were always in control. They would stop anything unlawful, just by being there.

He nervously approached the café. He thought he had seen Eileen with a tall beautiful woman, standing by the door. Admittedly, he noticed the beautiful woman first. He wanted to know who, or what, had been carried in to the café, and so had looked over there in expectation of some kind of revelation. Fear and other people stopped him from continuing his heroic step and storming in.

He signalled to Henry. 'Let's go to my shop.'

The words caused a flurry of interest to the groups that were mingling around him, and for a few seconds he was the centre of their attention again. He was the eyeball to their eyes, if that made sense. He could feel himself twitching. He wasn't having a full blown attack of nerves. That would come after the crowd threat had disappeared, the same as it usually did, but he was feeling like an arachnophobic again, one who had just spotted a very small dark shadow out of the corner of his eye. Arthur wondered if arachnophobics wore white socks. White socks were legendary for collecting little bits of this and that. He often found what looked like beetle legs on his. He couldn't imagine arachnophobics wearing them.

Distracting himself with other peoples fears seem to make him less terrified. He looked down, and started to slowly move through the squashed together bodies, while looking at the socks the people in front of him were wearing. He made it to the flower shop front, after counting ten pairs of white socks, three pairs of black socks and fourteen pairs of grey. Some of the white ones had muddy circles around the ankles, he noticed. The greys were a mixture of pattern and tones. He imagined arachnophobes mostly wore grey socks. Black wouldn't show the squashed remnants of the various species of the insect world stuck to the nylon underneath, that lulled the wearer into a false sense of security, but startled them when undressing. Grey would give warning, without being overly-finger pointing.

He opened the flower shop door with suppressed relief, shocking Rene into displaying her lap top screen saver at him.

She was always a bit weird too, he thought, as he shut the door behind Henry.

Chapter 10

The Switches were not particularly interested in the sky or Mrs. Lock.

They were interested in unlocked windows, and flippy pockets. Low slung jeans also had an interest for them, as did fashion magazines. Fashion magazines showed designer flaws that may give them access to personal belongings. They perused them with an unrealistic longing that someone would actually wear one of the advertised four-foot shoulder padded outfits, while hanging upside down from an over shiny plastic coated prop tree. It was a popular image in one issue.

Arthur was more aware of punks and hippies, with their strange arrangement of clothing. And he had his suspicions of Goths too. All their clothing was designed to attract attention, not for sexual attention, but to put words into others eyes.

Punks were nearly the same as himself, as witches, but used a louder medium than words, and a drugged, photosensitive epileptic to make their clothes. Safety pins were placed into strategic patterns and rip placements were designed with tatty dictorial thoughtfulness.

They weren't scary people like they presumed they were though.

The Switches kept away because they could see at a distance everything they needed to know.

Switches, after memorising the whole ensemble of bright materials, would convey to other Switches exactly what the wearer wanted them to convey.

Arthur hid behind a bunch or aromatic lilies and watched the

Switches stare at the door. They had already stared at the CTV, placed in the top right of the shop window, and at the frame of the window. They could take the glass out if they memorised where the frame nails were.

He had only observed them for a few minutes, but they had been looking at the shop since early morning, Rene had said. They had been staring at it individually, not en masse.

He looked at Rene. She couldn't see the café from the shop, and the savage trail had come into the village from the other end. He would have to look at the CTV tape to find out who, or what, they had carried into the café. One of the cameras, hidden upstairs, was angled in that direction.

With a courageous few steps he locked the shop door, before exiting through the side door, which led to the stairs.

Arthur had watched the CCTV video on quick time, and had breathed a sigh of relief. It was an old fat woman who had feinted. That was all. A badly dressed, overweight, grey haired woman had been carried into the café. Miranda had been helping the carriers, as was Graham, her boyfriend. It wasn't a cannibalistic orgy of gluttony after all. He stopped thinking of socks and took a peek at the rest of the fast forwarding scene.

A whole lot of people were looking at the sky and the Switches were making plans. They were obvious in their stance and hyper-eyed looks. On speeded up video the stance looked like a quick step dance as they leant against things, then didn't, and then did. Their feet shuffled in a bored, about-to-move way.

He quickly glanced at the videoed sky, before his crowd phobia returned. After the body fumbling symptoms of the phobia, he usually had jerky teeth, where his lips refused to move around. He didn't want to lose his vocal chords to a nervous reaction. He concentrated on the sky, hoping to relax himself into a state of calm, before returning to the shop.

He gazed, round eyed, at the speeded up videoed clouds. They looked like a hastily made cup of soya milked coffee. Soya milk curdled into shapes when he mixed it with a too hot cup of coffee. It made faces, like the sky, but unlike the sky, he never stared too long at the shapes that appeared in his cup. It was a hard sight for a vegan to swallow. No one liked big nosed milky men floating on top of their hot beverages. It sort of went against everything he believed in.

It turned his mid morning drink into a cauldron And it was gay. When he bent his head forward, to take a sip, it looked as if he was about to kiss a mirror.

And sliced bread did the same, when he stared at it. Images appeared just before he was about to eat it.

He mostly skipped breakfasts.

He re wound the tape further back, and looked for the clouds he and Henry had seen that morning, then fast forwarded it while pressing the play button. It was strange, but when he looked at them, the angel and face looked more like the number ten. He squinted his eyes. When the clouds were on fast forward, the morphing images were less noticeable as morphing images. They just looked like watery numbers. He fast forwarded again. The face appearing looked like a number nine, and the egg-timer like a number eight.

He felt like something important was about to happen. Years ago everything was announced in a 'count down' before some momentous event. It was the fashion to count backwards from ten, until one was reached. From what he could remember, after one, there were normally a lot of loud noises – fireworks and yelps, normally. Sometimes a few hysterical sharp laughs and applauses were thrown in. That was just the beginning of the event, but he couldn't remember what usually happened next. He would be too much in a state of frozen awareness.

The clouds, as far as he could remember, normally, at this time of the year, stopped at ten. There wasn't usually a quick and rapid nine and eight.

He stopped the tape at the white rectangles that had appeared in the sky and studied the scene. They looked like lost pixels, or an old film tape. Or, and most obviously, they looked like over sized snow. The rectangles were thin, long, and fuzzy, and out of season. He leant forward. They were number seven. The 'snow' couldn't be seen where the sun shone, only from above, and from one side.

How confusing. He turned the tape off and went down to the shop. Henry would know more. He had studied the baby X phenomenon. He knew about weather patterns. He had also organized flower shows for Arthur, so knew all about momentous occasion arranging and counting backwards.

Henry was staring out of the window. They had been followed. A taller, skinnier, stronger looking Miranda was standing in the road, looking about her. It was good that Arthur kept his windows clean, as she hadn't been able to see him in the reflecting surface, but she was worrying Henry. He dived behind the specialty grasses, and peeled his coat off. It was a reversible puffa jacket, with the puffa only shown on one side. He turned it inside out, and hoped it would suffice in confusing the woman.
Rene was still hiding behind her laptop. The screen faced the crowd outside and she was bent, behind the lid.
Crowd phobia probably was a family genetic thing, he thought. The jacket was damp next to his skin. He looked at the Miranda double with resentment. Switches were so inconvenient. But, and he reddened at his thoughts, she did look tidier than Miranda, and her skin looked more like how he imagined a grand daughter. He peeked at her again. Perhaps she would be a good Switch.
Henry felt his leg spasm.
He signed, in an exasperated way and bent over to inspect his legs. Three times in one day meant he was well on his way to

194

being a zombie servant.

☼

The café owner banged on the counter.
'If you are not buying, you can't stay.' He said, looking at the
packed café with a hint of disgust. They had put the bag lady on
the tables, as if it was her bed, and hadn't even asked him for
permission. She would have a coffee stain on her bum, and he
would have buckled table legs.
The people in the café looked confusedly at each other but also
with a hint of eager agreement. Of course, they seemed to imply,
why didn't they think of that? Of course they were waiting to
purchase something. Give them a moment or two, they hinted.
The café owner had seen it all before. This crowd obviously
knew each other. He could tell by their half –finished expressions
and noiseless instant queuing. He changed his mind. He wasn't
going to start an argument with them about acceptable table
manners.

'I'll have one.'
'Me too'
'Mine's hot chocolate with sugar.'
'Mines tea, with two.'
'Skimmed milk in mine, please,'
'I'll have coffee.'
'Coffee, de-caffinated. One sugar in mine.'
The café owner stopped moving. 'Anyone else?' He asked
sullenly.
'Well, I prefer herbal, but just week tea with no sugar or milk
will be fine.'
'I prefer my herbal sweetened with honey, if you have any.'

The café owner edged backwards into the kitchen, before anyone
else could place their order.

195

The awkwardness was probably not deliberate. They were probably emphasizing to each other that they were individual, even though they looked the same. Each would know they were not standing next to a Switch.

He preferred Switches. With Switches all he would have had to do was make a big pot of tea. As long as they were all doing the same thing, they were quite happy. They could relax their nosiness. One soup was also sufficient. It saved them all investigating each others dietary habits, for when one of them switched.

'Nettle tea, please.' Another one called after him.

Miranda supposed that Mrs. Lock had felt the attention leave her. Some people thought attention gave others a sort of static electric charge. They just seemed to know when it wasn't there anymore.

Mrs. Lock's eyes had flickered at the noise. A bourbon biscuit appeared on her cheek. Another one, a digestive, balanced under her ear. It had the word 'digestive' written on it.

Miranda jumped as one of the observers grabbed his camera, and called out, 'around here quick' while staring at Mrs. Lock's blouse cuff. The biscuit under Mrs. Lock's ear broke in half, and an image of a hand offered Miranda some of it, in an instant, two dimensional hand movement.

She looked at it warily while some men huddled to one side of Mrs. Lock's wrist.

It was unusual for Mrs. Lock. She hardly ever used emergency font. She had no need to. Nothing was ever an emergency, because emergencies were so regular, it was like they had been planned. It rained and land flooded at regular times. Fires hardly

196

ever happened and fire engines only appeared on fire work night. The emergency services thought of changing their name to 'slow moving observers' because of it.

Mrs. Lock, subconsciously, like when she was asleep, thought her skin was absolutely wonderful. She was over awed by it's ability to project pictures on to her skin, and was even more impressed by her almost autistic ability to calculate most mathematics problems. As her face biscuited up, her subconscious was calculating air pressure and radio frequencies. It noted minuscule drops in wind speed, and averaged the temperatures of the last thirty years.

Her arm, the bit that showed from her cuff, had a panicking look to the emergency font, as if it was shaking. The font was a red colour, and was like it was scratched on. It was loud for a skin image. The words spelt 'Alarm! Alarm!'

Next to it was an image of the Emblem Seal. A horizontal line passed through each segment of it, in a measuring type way. The table opposite was reflected on the hump of her thumb, and showed the letters 'GZK' in the ten o' clock position. At the three o clock position was a string of folded spaghetti, and a crispy and crumbly breaded mushroom shape leaned against her index finger. A directional line led from each table icon to each segment of the Emblem Seal.

Mrs. Lock, totally unaware, was drawing a remote key diagram. A 'remote key' was computer speak for something that unlocks a computer or radio frequency.

A thoughtful on looker leant over and pressed a red spot that had appeared next to the alarmed skin, which responded by shrinking the font until it disappeared. .

The accumulated amateur photographers gawped in an appropriate manner when the emergency font was replaced by an Arial font, which clearly stated that they had to find the emblem seal and turn on the wi-fi.

Her skin then cleared, and waited.

197

On this occasion her skin was as clear as Eileen's was, and nobody quite understood the pictograms.

The wind outside forced a gust through the village. The gust was stronger than the last, and caused the crowd to spontaneously grab at each other, in an attempt not to fall over.
The wind speed was a shock. A wheel barrow moved a couple of inches, and a bike fell over.
The crowd pushed against it, and the Switches looked for dropped things.
A few held onto lampposts, and some hid around corners.
Eileen flung herself past Miss. Runes, who was standing in the door way when the gust blew through.
Miss. Runes hardly felt it. She had turned her head so the air lifted her hair in an appropriate and beautiful way. It streamed and shone as she accidentally looked down the High Street. The road in the middle was clearing rapidly and only the giants let the gust pass by un-noticed. They stared at the sky, obliviousl to the commotion around them. Miss. Runes looked at them and waited for admiration.

The wind speed picking up coincided with the taller Miranda spotting Henry in the shop window. He would have stayed hidden by reflecting grey people and Switches, but they were now crammed in to nearby shops. The flower shop was still locked.
Henry had been by the window, looking up at the sky with concentration, when the taller Miranda had seen him. Arthur was standing next to him, with Rene's laptop in his hands. He had downloaded a few images of the clouds to show Henry, who had

agreed that the images were hiding numbers. Ominous count down numbers.

Henry had squinted his eyes, and had stood by the window, trying to look past to the clouds, just as the gust took most of the crowd, and the taller Miranda, away.

The clouds were strangely not moving, like they should be. They were steadfast, despite the rapidly increasing wind speed.

He looked at them curiously.

'Number six'. He said with a side long look at Arthur.

Arthur moved to the other side of Henry, and stared at the sky. There was an image of a baby reading a book. The baby was very small and the book was very big. It had morphed out of the egg-timer shape, which had slowly changed when they weren't looking.

If the two men had thought to inspect each other they would have noticed that Henry's chest had changed, as had Arthur's ankle, to images that they had never seen before. The letters appearing in reaction to the clouds above were hidden in the same arty disguise on their bodies. The images that appeared on them were almost identical to each other. It was probably because they had a lot in common, and thought the same way.

 Book of words;
There used to be TV programs that asked strangers, who were in different rooms, to draw, on to paper, what the other person was thinking. It was a test of telepathic communication. Subject A would be asked to think of something, and subject B was asked to draw it. Nearly all the experiments had a hundred percent success, because every object in the entire world is made up of circles and lines. Subject A would, for example, think of a train, and all subject B had to do was draw a line and a circle. That would imply that he had telepathically received at least part of the message.

Far from being hailed as an idiot the programmer director received grants, for further research, because of the high percentage of success.

Witches were almost certain that the program content had been changed to stop fights breaking out on public transport as the real question was not whether strangers could tell what another stranger was thinking, without looking at each other, but whether skin-talkers were aware of their own skin; whether they were consciously sending messages to their skin, or whether it was an outside source that the skin reacted to.

Experiments, not shown on the telly, in the past, was to show a skin-talker a drawing and to see if it was reproduced on the skin by the skin-talker concentrating on the drawing. The drawings were normally simple shapes – a star, parallel lines, circles and a square.

This was an important area of research for those that worried whether radio frequency interfered with the bodies own electrical signals, and also whether the skin talkers frequently offended others, on purpose, by showing insulting caricatures on their skin.

If it was outside interference, then it might mean superior surveillance, extreme power and probably beings of physical superiority was having a laugh at them.

If it was the skin talkers themselves, the Head of Medical research and the Head of the BBC was going to duff one of the skin talkers up, the next time they saw an unflattering caricature of themselves on their skin .

By the time the question reached the program- maker it had changed it to the less controversial and less damaging question of whether telepathy existed.
This was safer than finding out if superior surveillance, extreme power and probably beings of physical superiority were out there.

Henry's chest had a display of an emu, and on Arthur's leg was a smaller emu, which was more like a skinny chicken.
Chickens, in Arthur's opinion *were* overfed miniature emus. He couldn't understand why anyone would want to eat the zoo exhibits, and avoided supermarkets. He was convinced that the miniature emus had been left to wander about in England by genetic scientists, centuries before, hoping to improve the economics of the little island by giving it some kind of difference to other places. England was a perfect place for that type of thing.
They were both number sixes though.
If Henry and Arthur had thought about their skin patterns before, in relation to cloud disguises, they may have realized that all the images that had appeared on their skin, over the years, since they were born, were disguised numbers or letters and the same as the sky.
It probably wasn't an important fact, but would have made their lives a bit more interesting - it would have been like playing scrabble, very, very, slowly.

Arthur wondered if his phobia of people should be expanded to include clouds. He was beginning to have the same reaction to them. The wind gusts had frightened him. He had seen hurricane racked towns, and didn't think it would be beneficial to experience it during the actual event. Perhaps he could hide under the shop counter, as Rene was doing. He could see the window glass tremble. Henry hadn't seen it.

☼

Book of words;
Morris dancers were thought to be the first weather
forecasters. Their hankies were wind speed predictors, the
bells were rain warners, the bigger bells, strapped on the
inside of the knee, were flood warnings, and the Morris
dancer hats were sun cautions.

The only problem with their forecasting was that it wasn't an
actual forecast, and more of a 'here and now' experience. If
anyone looked out of the window they could see, just with a
glance in their direction, what weather defense clothing
would be needed for the next few minutes. Morris dancers
weren't noted for their long term predications. They were
useful for new comers though, as the weather hardly ever
varied, so their flying knees and thumping sticks were
recorded for the following years. Thumping sticks were
thunder.

Later Morris dancers learnt to adapt their jigglings to match
an actual predicted weather warning, as broadcasted by the
radio. They made little aisles, and danced down them with
statistical and thoughtful steps, to show wind speed, stopping
when needed, to bang their cymbals together.

Mrs. Locks head showed hankies flying and cow bells across her
cheeks. Her urgency had not been acted upon. She thought that
she may not have been understood. She was in a village, where
modern day living had been hidden under checked table cloths.
Laptops, she had noticed, were ready to use but stashed in table
cutlery draws.
The sign of the Morris dancers meant a here and now request she

202

had thought, to villagers.

She was still asleep. The other side of her face showed a three layered cake, with a serving slice, and a table cloth pulled up, to show a cutlery draw.

Several people, who saw the image, looked under the tables, and rose, shaking their heads. Several people took the image as a sign to protect themselves from the wind by sitting under the tables, and complied. The weather was getting worse, which wasn't what they had expected.

The people around Mrs. Lock had been trying to connect to the internet. The two gift presenters were sheltered in the local bakery.

Graham looked around at the fast moving audience, some of who had quickly ducked under the nearby tables. The radiation problem wasn't that bad. It wasn't as if Mrs. Lock was a nuclear bomb or anything like that, but he could see their point. The air could carry some of the radio waves in their direction. It would probably be harmless if it wasn't for her bacteria. Her bacteria may be thought-laden. They may be splattered with a yearning for a cup of coffee, or, from where he could see, a biscuit.

He wondered if her fat was radio active too. It would be like his imaginary flobs he supposed. He stepped back and looked around. The last gust of wind had made a far off cracking sound. He looked at the door and reddened. The beautiful woman was looking beautiful, by the door frame.

Chapter 11

There was an almost unnoticeable movement by the counter of the café. A laptop, previously being used to calculate plastic spoon costs, silently glowed it's Wi-Fi receiver button.

Mrs. Lock smiled in her sleep. Her bags, still sat on the chair, made a rustling sound in a coincidental and parallel way. Miss. Runes had blocked most of the wind with her body, and Eileen had contributed to the draught excluder effect by passing by her. Only a little of the wind penetrated the café. It was enough, though, to upset the symmetry of the hand bag. The bag fell over and opened. The emblem box dropped from it and fell onto Mrs. Lock's chest. It rolled off into the folds of her neck before the emblem seal fell out.

 She felt it, but it wasn't enough to wake her up. A shadow of it appeared on her jowl instead, shaped like a lighthouse. It wasn't a real shadow. It was a faux shadow, with faux light beams emanating from it. The folds on her neck changed to look like tides on a beach, and her skin added a couple of flying number '3's in a flying bird type effect.

A change also occurred on her forehead and caused Miranda to peer closer. Mrs. Lock's skin was forming the number five. The baby shape, that had been the number six grew, and looked closer at a page. The image slightly turned, so it now looked like the number five. It would only look like the number five to those that were looking for numbers.

Mrs. Lock had been lucky. The number five rhymed with 'alive' so her subconscious had tried to revive her, in a congenial longing to share. She was still asleep but she knew. All she had to do was wait.

The Emblem seal was the catalyst.

She had thought, while looking at it outside, that there was something electrical about it. Something static and modern hidden in its hierarchic form. She had thought she had seen tiny glints and molten metal.

When she had turned it round, she must have turned it on. It was as if she had been given instruction of how to use it, without being aware of the learning.

She must have picked up the information from walking along the street.

It was the same when she stood around outside electrical shops. She knew, without a sound being made, exactly what a cyclonal 50 remittance machine was, and how to operate a gauge rater. The customers just couldn't stop conveying information. With electricians it was mostly hand movements made into descriptive nuances.

If she had been awake, she wouldn't have remembered a thing about it, but while asleep, she knew, with certainty, it would stop the storm from happening. If it could connect to the Wi-Fi, then it could transmit the radio frequencies it had found outside. It was a transfiguration key, she was pretty sure of it.

Another gust of wind, that was stronger than the previous, shot through the village. There were a couple of bangs and a bike flew down the road. The crowds stood back from their perspective shop windows and held their breath. Their cameras were aimed with renewed interest at the scenes outside. Most of them were paper people, and never really took an interest in village types of lives. They have never seen wind down a country lane before. There weren't, like Graham had presumed, radio-logistics type of people. Most of them weren't anyway. Only one or two of the crowd were involved in radio frequency study and recognized, like Graham did, the GZK abbreviation.

The photo of Mrs. Lock's skin had been hastily shown around the room, where it was compared to the sugar patterns that had been on the hill. Several people had walked over to the table and had taken photos of the mess left there too. Astonishment mixed with despair showed on most faces. They just didn't know what it all meant; the wind was increasing and Mrs. Lock was still asleep.

Mrs. Lock grimaced in her sleep. Nothing had happened. The emblem had nestled on her neck, but she could sense that the clouds were blowing backwards. She could feel the clouds up turn, as if they were her tongue, and she felt a chilled awareness down her spine. The rain, when it came, would be ferocious. The country seemed to be collecting the static waste of the continents. The oceans had thrown the polarized air up north, and it was probably collecting on the edge of Greenland, ready to throw it back down. Mrs. Lock snored.

The biscuit on Mrs. Lock's neck developed teeth marks, and Miranda watched with fascination as the page the baby was reading grew bigger. The corner of the page was turned, as if it was bookmarked. Writing appeared on the page.

The turned corner was a disguised number four.

The next burst of wind bent trees and moved rubbish bins. Some smaller windows broke and a shed door flew past.

The accumulated crowd froze, and she stood further back in their mixed shelters.

The flower shop window cracked and broke.

Arthur and Henry run to the dividing door, calling at Rene as they did so. They were lucky the wind was pulling and not pushing. Most of the glass was dragged outside. The shops contents were lifted up, and thrown in the air as they slammed the dividing door.

When the emblem seal dropped from the chair, on to Mrs. Lock's neck, the onlookers felt relief. Something was happening that was good. They stopped trying to loosen the cloth around Mrs. Lock's bottom, which may or may not have been a squashed pocket, and one of them reached forward. He was about to pick the emblem off her neck when he noticed the sea scene she had created. It was like a miniature painting, and he didn't want to disturb her. He beckoned the others to look at her.

Cameras were clicked.

Some of the Switches hastily pocketed other things that had dropped from the bag. They collected anything and everything that may be useful to them later on. A used bus ticket, a napkin and a library card was swiftly grasped. One of them grabbed Mrs. Locks other bag and moved the chair, which had covered her head, back to the floor.

Mrs. Lock's bus ticket would be ironed out and kept to use when the date coincided with the one on the ticket. A bit of thumb maneuvering may be used, but it was still free transport.

They knew all about forgery, about using a scanner, about altering photos with a photo computer program and printing out their own bus ticket, but that wasn't the point. Someone else had paid for their stolen ticket, and it gave them satisfaction in knowing this. They had made no effort at all, so felt superior.

The grey haired people warily took sneaky photos of the pocketers, while hiding their heads from possible debris.

They could hear wood splinter, and could hear rubbish, left at the back of the café, hit against walls. A sneaky plug socket manoeuvrer took a brave lunge at the gas tap, quickly turning it to the off position, before making a brave attempt to turn the electric appliances off. He left the computer plugged in but shoved the laptop under the counter. He rolled across the floor and unplugged a selection of Argos must-haves, before trying the door that led to the back kitchen.

It was locked. The cafe owner had decided that he didn't want to confront the multitude of wanters of mixed hot drinks and had hid himself upstairs, after locking the door. The wind had also scared him into his top room. He hid behind stores of polystyrene cups and paper napkins, while breathing heavily.

Mrs. Lock was left looking as if she was on her own. Her body looked like a giant pie. She was unaware of her fatness but did not wear frilly blouses because she sort of knew what she looked like to others. Frilly cuffs on fat people looked like pie rims. Especially if they were lying down and belly-button exposed. She had seen inside a pie shop, and knew it was true. Belly buttons were in the middle of crusts. She avoided those pie shops that had metal handles on either end of the pie tin. It was one of her aversions. Her dreamy thoughts were showing on her face again. She was thinking of the clowns that used to dress in a split costume – one side black, and one side white, that would fall backwards into the arms of their friends. They were, she supposed ready, take away pies.

Her face showed two long thin rectangles, falling down her

cheek. One side was black, one side was white.

The wind calmed. Some quick thinkers grabbed hold of nearby tables and started to stack them in front of the café window. One braved the weather and looked for a pull down shutter on the outside.

 Mrs. Lock was still oblivious. They peered closer, and then turned their cameras on again.

The camera flashes surprised them. It had grown dark, as the shutter was pulled down, and the quick burst of light slightly blinded them. They maneuvered themselves around Mrs. Lock's face, which had responded to the light with little squares of icons.

The cloud on her forehead was still hiding a number four. Miranda looked closer at the writing that appeared in the cloud page that the baby was holding. 'Verasity = 397gzks ^ / 5921'.

She had had to squint her eyes to see that one. She hastily pulled out her own camera, and zoomed in on it. She would find out what it meant later.

A commuter type person nodded at her approvingly, and then edged her away from Mrs. Lock's face, so he could take a photo at a better angle. It was like she was at a musical festival, and Mrs. Lock was the main act, or, when applied to Mrs. Lock, the main fat. Miranda tried to look at him annoyed, but he didn't notice.

He pointedly turned his back on her, and zoomed down at the emblem seal, moving around it like a fashion photographer, until he was underneath it. His camera seemed to be better equipped for Mrs. Lock photography than the rest, because he suddenly looked a little more interested in what he was taking pictures of. He picked up the emblem seal, to the annoyance of the other onlookers, and turned it upside down.

Hidden in the intaglio relief of the deer was the same letters as Mrs. Lock was showing. The leg of it made up the 'G', the hoof and the grass beneath made up the 'Z', and the 'K' the head and antlers.

The emblem filled with sudden energy.

The light from the camera flashes had re-charged the battery that no one knew it had. The Gzk began to transmit.

The Switches were obvious, when they were caught on camera. The café owner looked up, from his hiding place of cardboard boxes, and watched the scene downstairs. His misgivings about the grey clothed people were forgotten, as he saw them barricade the window and turn off the electric. They were a responsible law abiding group of thugs. They reminded him of Chinese tourists; always eager, in the past, to buy his old fashioned forgotten film cameras, knowing that they photographed the truth. Digital ones just didn't capture the light, they said. They were like them, but without their little pocket Tamagochis.

He couldn't see the fascination they all had for the fat woman though.

They were all taking photos of her, even though the sky had fallen on top of them. Perhaps it was an impromptu fashion shoot to tempt weary old ladies in to garden centre buying.

He could see by looking at the screen which people were the Switches. They had an obvious dishonest and ugly look to them, that couldn't be hidden by a new haircut or clothes. They looked desperate. They were looking with envy and greed at the emblem seal.

The photographer turned the emblem seal the right way up and looked at the sterling top. He smirked at the symbols. It was a film set extra, stolen probably. It wasn't much, but represented oldness. Engraved on the sterling top was a sleeping eye. Only the eyelid showed. With curled eye lashes. Behind it was a quarter moon, with two lines stuck through it. Then there were waves, or what looked like waves, next to it. A few more symbols, that had to be looked at closer, was followed by an open eye. A horses head was apparent, in a Norse type of style. He pulled the emblem back. The images turned into script writing. The letters spelt 'Rom', Mrs. Lock's first name, and also the name of a part in a computer. Read Only Memory.

 He wrinkled his eyebrow.

The flowers flew past the window in a seemingly co-coordinating approach. They danced and streamed, as if the snowy rectangles of a few minutes before had slimmed down and fallen backwards, leaving themselves as thin white stalks.

They sort of fitted the occasion, as when the wind suddenly dropped the sky had reached the number three. The flowers, still being symbolic and coincidental, showed missing petals and three petal stems as they fell to the ground.

An open round cloud had appeared by the sun, mimicking it perfectly. A cloud drifted in front of the sun, making it look like the other part of a number three.

The rainbow was slowly fading.

Some of the Switches looked at it in awe. Two suns were their symbol of righteousness.

Two is one, they started to chant.

But, luckily, only with their eyes.

If anyone was standing in front of them they would have been stunned by the eye-loudness and co-ordination of their words.

Mrs. Lock thought that the Switches were only silent talkers to trap people who pretended they were omnipresence. The bogus deity had to pop back round corners to make sure there was a crowd of people cheering at them, and that they hadn't imagined it, thereby showing they weren't an ominpresence. The cheering, of course, was silent cheering.

Mrs. Lock woke up.

She sat up, with a sort of bend and twist action, while looking at the photographer. On her cheek was an image of a topless woman. It was the number three, disguised.

The assorted crowd clapped for no reason at all, and the topless woman on her cheek looked as if she had blushed with pleasure but Mrs. Lock had reddened while trying to catch her breathe, unaware of what her cheek was portraying.

Miss. Runes was looking at her with split eyes, and Eileen was spotting at her. She looked around. Graham was standing back, with a look of embarrassment, while wondering how Mrs. Lock knew what he had been thinking. Miranda was turning, ready to greet her grandmother. Lots of people felt relieved for no apparent reason, and the photographer was handing Mrs. Lock the emblem seal back. She took it with a reluctant hand. It probably *did* belong to the tall woman that was introducing herself to Miranda, but she was going to keep it for now, until the old couple asked for it back. She felt a strange affinity with the emblem. She curled her fingers around it tightly, and swung herself slowly off the tables.

The assorted crowd suddenly remembered that they never approached Mrs. Lock, and that they were never obvious. They slowly slipped their cameras and phones back into their pockets and moved the tables back to their café-use positions. One wiped the centre tables. Most of them left.

They sunk into side roads and foot paths so quickly and silently that it was as if the wind had sucked them out.

Mrs. Lock put her head down, squeezed passed the door way, and passed Eileen. She spared a glance for Miranda's grandmother, who she slightly remembered passing in the street.

She was lucky that she had got out of the cafe alive. She shuddered. When she thought about it, perhaps they were about to have her for dinner. Placing her on a makeshift table was kind of like treating her like an overgrown turkey. Why hadn't they taken her to the church, or waited for the obligatory ambulance that is normally waiting in the side lines at organized events like she had just witnessed?

It was lucky she had woken up in time. Miranda's grandmother had been standing by the door, with the angry but beautiful woman, which was a bad omen.

And Graham had been looking at her as if she was a liar.

Mrs. Lock shrugged and put on her hat. Keeping her head down, she carefully walked though the dropped flowers, and made her way home, pausing only to glance at the flower shop window on the opposite side of the road. She barely noticed that the corner of the glass was still attached to the window frame, creating a number four, and that the other witches or Switches were no where to be seen.

The end

www.ingramcontent.com/pod-product-compliance
Lightning Source LLC
Chambersburg PA
CBHW060806120626
46557CB00001B/106